Of Graves, Worms and Epitaphs

Of Graves, Worms and Epitaphs

TOBIAS WELLS

PUBLISHED FOR THE CRIME CLUB BY
Doubleday
NEW YORK
1988

All of the characters in this book
are fictitious, and any resemblance
to actual persons, living or dead,
is purely coincidental.

Library of Congress Cataloging-in-Publication Data

Forbes, Stanton, 1923–
    Of graves, worms and epitaphs / Tobias Wells. — 1st ed.
        p.   cm.
    I. Title.
PS3556.06703 1988
813′.54—dc19   87-33967
                                                              CIP

OG

To those I love best . . . Bill, of course,
and Dan and Anne and Andy.
To Cheri and Joe and Julie
and the newer breed,
Derek and Ashley, Christopher and Patricia,
little Drew and
Michaela or Kyle so be it

Let's talk of graves, of worms and
    epitaphs;
Make dust our paper, and with rainy eyes
Write sorrow on the bosom of the earth.
Let's choose executers
    and talk of wills.

King Richard II
Act III, Scene II
William Shakespeare

Of Graves, Worms and Epitaphs

It was a new architectural complex. Brick cottages with tile roofs and window walls of glass looked out on a tranquil lake. Underground sprinklers dampened newly cut lawns, and bright umbrellas bloomed like giant zinnias on secluded patios in the summer sunlight.

The central roadway, bordered by elms and maples and weeping willows, was marked at its wide entrance with a tasteful quarterboard sign, the letters cut deep, gold on black. "Shangri-la" it read, and beneath that, in smaller script, "The Retirement Village."

A black Chrysler turned onto the roadway and paused briefly at the sign before continuing on. The car was so highly polished that the sun made moons on its surfaces. There were four people inside. The driver wore a civilian suit; the other three, two men and a woman, wore police uniforms.

Officer Alice Buono was telling Wellesley Police Chief Knute Severson that Shangri-la was only a little more than a year old.

"I didn't even know it was here," Lieutenant Mark Beavers confessed.

"It's on the old Howe estate." Sergeant Gil Tracy's comment was gratuitous; Severson knew the locale. He grunted in response and braked the car in a neatly lined parking place in front of the largest building, identified in black and gold as "The Center." Sergeant Tracy was responsible for the automobile's appearance, maintenance and theoretically, the driving of it. Chief Severson preferred to drive himself; in fact he preferred to drive his own Mustang. But today, on official business, he took the Chrysler. It ran well, it was practically new and he liked the way it handled. He felt, however, even though it was designated as the chief's car it was too ostentatious—well, more like dignified, formal, funereal . . . hell, stuffy, that was the word for the Chrysler. Old? A car for the elderly?

Everybody got out, four doors slammed shut and at that signal the heavy oak door of The Center opened, and a slender young woman stood in the doorway. Knute almost expected her to be wringing her hands but she seemed, from this distance at least, quite controlled. The quartet walked toward her, careful to keep to the sidewalk. There were no "Keep off the grass" signs but there might as well have been.

"Miss Evans?" asked Knute, watching the expression in her clear blue eyes.

"Yes, I'm Fancy Evans. Please come in."

Knute hoped his eyebrows didn't betray him but apparently they did because she colored beneath her tan. "I know," she said, "my mother was frivolous."

They followed Fancy Evans through a foyer tastefully furnished with grandfather clock, misty oil paintings and a cream-and-blue Oriental carpet. An arch on the right opened onto a large, open room dotted with sofas and chairs placed in intimate groupings. The heart of the area was marked by an oversized fieldstone fireplace, and the focal point was a giant television screen.

A similar arch on the left led to a dining room of equal size. Round tables, each with four chairs, were spaced far enough apart to allow a certain amount of privacy. The color scheme was beige and brown with touches of gray. Very subdued, thought Knute. Very elegant. Very expensive.

"This way," said Miss Evans, moving between the tables, past a cafeteria-style arrangement of steam tables, through a swinging door and into a large stainless steel and chrome kitchen. It was, as were the other rooms, deserted.

"In here." Fancy Evans reached for the handle of one of the stainless steel doors. "I didn't move anything," she said, stepping aside so they could enter. "I could see she was dead so I knew there wasn't anything I could do. You can see for yourselves . . ." And they could.

Chief Severson had seen his share of dead bodies but he had never seen a frozen human before. He knelt, his breath creating a small smoke screen, and looked at the woman. She lay on her side, curled in a fetal position—for warmth, no doubt. Her eyes were open; they looked colorless. Her mouth was open too. Set in a cry for help, perhaps?

The pink lipstick was smeared, the blond hair mussed. Her hands, curled into fists, were blood-flecked. She wore white slacks and a pink-and-white cotton blouse and on her feet were pink, plastic slippers. The outfit was a young woman's. Severson estimated her age at sixty? Seventy? Maybe more?

His knees creaked as he rose. "Where is everybody?" he asked Fancy Evans. "Shouldn't there be people in the kitchen, in the dining room? Shouldn't someone have heard her?"

"Most of the staff is on vacation," she told him, "and most of the residents are on an Alaskan cruise. This is our summer routine. It enables our people to have a proper holiday."

It was bone-chilling cold in the walk-in freezer. Alice Buono's teeth were chattering. "Let's go outside," Knute suggested. "Dr. Bell will be here directly. No need for us to catch pneumonia. Gil, there should be a couple of raincoats in the trunk of the car, right? You and Mark can wear them while you check this place out." He turned to the Evans woman. "Any idea how she got in the freezer? Would she go in there on her own? Officer

Buono, bring your notebook and we'll sit at one of the tables in the dining area. Miss Evans is going to tell us all about—what was her name? Roseanna dela Mare? All about Roseanna dela Mare. Any family?"

The deceased was the widow of Arnold dela Mare—did Chief Severson recognize the name? Something about frozen foods, wasn't it? Yes, frozen fish products. He'd been the innovator—a natural with that name, right? He'd made a fortune in seafood and Roseanna had inherited it all. She was in her late seventies and if she looked younger it was because she took very good care of herself, not to mention the magic touch of skilled plastic surgeons. She was survived by a son, Gordon dela Mare.

"Have you notified the next of kin?"

Fancy Evans shook her head. "He's on vacation. Driving across the country. We're trying to reach him. His secretary is on his trail. We did reach his ex-wife. She's the mother of Roseanna's only granddaughter." She looked remorseful. "I keep thinking, what a dreadful way to die. Not that any way is a good way. But freezing to death. Just like her husband's fish." She laughed, a nervous titter.

Dr. Bell arrived and went to work. Sergeant Tracy went out to the car that the doctor came in and brought back Officer Barnes and a stretcher.

"You said the place is practically deserted," Knute reminded Fancy Evans. "But you're here and there must be others."

"Yes, of course." She watched the stretcher pass by. "I'm here because I'm Mr. Bancroft's assistant. He is the administrator, as you know. He's on his vacation, too; he's in London right now. I've sent him a cable. It's a shame. He works so hard; it's not easy running Shangri-la; it's such a quality place and it takes constant attention . . . I'm sorry, I'm rambling, aren't I? I'm here to cover for Mr. Bancroft and when he returns, then I go on holiday. That is, I'm supposed to go on holiday, but now . . ." Her voice trailed off, then strengthened. "Lulu Greer is on duty in the kitchen. She has a couple of temporary girls to give her a hand but since there are only five of the villagers in residence—"

"Villagers?"

"We call those who live here villagers. It's so much nicer than retirees or seniors or golden-agers, don't you think? It gives them a sense of real community; that's what Mr. Bancroft thinks. And since we do have elections, we're very democratic . . . I'm rambling again. You want to know who's here—well, there's—there *was* Mrs. dela Mare and there's Mr. Butler, that's Mr. Edward Butler, he likes to be called Ward; Miss Delilah Ventress, surely you've heard of her—well, you probably don't read romance novels but maybe your wife does (if you're married that is). Delilah Ventress writes very successful romance novels."

Officer Buono asked how to spell Ventress. Apparently she didn't read romance novels either. Miss Evans spelled, then continued.

"Mr. Cullingham, William Cullingham he is, he has—*had* the cottage next to Roseanna's, they're—*were*—quite friendly; he'll take it very hard, I fear. I haven't told any of the villagers yet but I'll have to tell them soon because they'll wonder about the police vehicles—"

She was cut off in mid-sentence by the appearance of a woman in a wheelchair who motor-propelled herself into the dining room. "What's going on, Miss Evans?" The questioner had a deep voice for so small a person. Alice Buono wrote "rusty voice" in her notebook. "What are the police doing here? What's happened?"

Fancy Evans stood up and clasped her hands in front of her,

all composure suddenly gone. "Oh, Mrs. Meeny," she cried, "Mrs. dela Mare is dead."

"Is that all?" She wheeled her chair closer. She had a tanned and weathered face, and her eyes made tiny slits above puffy cheeks. "No, that isn't all, is it? You wouldn't call the cops just because one of us old fossils kicked the bucket. What happened? Some camel with a broken back did her in? Has Roseanna dela Mare been murdered?"

Knute Severson looked at her over his new bifocal lenses. "It's possible," he said.

Mrs. Meeny smiled a bright, porcelain smile. "It couldn't have happened to a better person," she said.

Buono took her statement:

Evangeline Marie Meeny, that's me. Age seventy-eight, weight one hundred and forty-nine to one hundred and fifty-five depending, gray hair, eyes ditto, distinguishing marks: curvature of the spine but I get around just fine in my mechanized go-cart.

I'm a widow with a rich son, that's what I'm doing in this la-de-dah place. Not that I'm knocking it, you understand. If you gotta go, go first-class, that's my motto, and this place is just about as first-class as you can get.

I didn't go with the rest of them to Alaska because wheelchairs don't work as well on ships as they do on airplanes. My son, Roger, is taking me to the Caribbean this Christmas. He's renting a house and taking the whole family. I've got four grandsons and we're going to have a real family holiday, which suits me better than any cruise to Alaska.

My cottage is across Alpha square from Roseanna's. They've got these little squares, you see, and there are six cottages per square. Figure it like a clock, if you want to—say Roseanna's place is at noon, mine's at six. Bill Cullingham's at one o'clock. We're the only three in residence, as they say, at this time. From Alpha square, I mean. Old Ward Butler is around, too, Rhett's what I call him, he's on the other side in Delta square and so is Delilah Ventress from the next square, Beta. So I guess if somebody locked Roseanna in the freezer you've got to figure it was one of us. And we're all a little off in the upper story, so take your pick.

Knute picked her up on that. "How did you know she was locked in the freezer?"

Evangeline Meeny's squinty eyes blazed for a moment. "A little bird told me," she said and cackled.

The door to the freezer was double-width, of a heavy stainless steel, both slick and smooth. It fastened firmly on the outside with a pivoting handle that fitted snugly into its catch. The sealing gasket cushioned its close. There was no mechanism inside but there was a safety device, Fancy Evans explained. "A red light comes on out here in the kitchen when someone's inside. See?" And she pointed to a bulb above the door.

Knute opened the door, stepped inside and looked out. "It isn't working," he said.

She looked troubled. "No." She thought a moment. "Maybe the bulb burned out."

"Have you got a stepladder?" The light was too high to reach without something to stand on.

"Yes, I think so. Oh, there you are, Lulu." She spoke to a heavyset woman in a white uniform who had appeared in the kitchen entranceway. "Could you get Chief Severson a stepladder? Where have you been anyway?"

Lulu Greer gave Fancy Evans a sullen look. "Home, of course. I don't start lunch until ten-thirty." She looked at a watch on her thick wrist. "And that's about what it is now. What's going on in my kitchen?"

"I'm Chief Severson," Knute started to explain but Miss Evans interrupted.

"It's Roseanna dela Mare. Somebody shut her up in the frozen food locker."

"Christ," exclaimed Lulu, "is she dead?"

"Like a frozen mackerel." Evangeline Meeny put in her two cents' worth.

"How about the ladder?" Knute asked patiently. Lulu brought it, muttering, and he climbed up to look at the red light bulb. Handkerchief in hand, he gave it a quick twist and it came on, indicating that Beavers and Tracy were still inside the cold room.

"The bulb was loose?" Fancy Evans waved her hands. "How awful! It could have saved her life."

Knute put his handkerchief away. Tracy would take fingerprints. He should find something. You had to reach through a metal cage to turn the bulb and the spaces were so narrow it had been difficult to get his wrapped fingers inside. Chances were, he thought, they'd have a remorseful murderer by the end of the day. He could just imagine how boring it must be living in a place like Shangri-la. Everybody dating from the same decade, petty problems became big issues. There was nothing else to worry about except when you were going to die and you'd fight to see that that wasn't tomorrow. How calculating can you be at seventy or eighty? he wondered. The mind wasn't as sharp as it used to be. His mind, for instance. He was getting forgetful about some things and he was only in his forties.

Bill Cullingham, Ward Butler, Delilah Ventress. He'd go to them now, he decided. Tracy and Beavers could finish up here; Officer Buono would go with him to take notes. She was a godsend. He'd always hated note-taking. Half the time he couldn't read his own writing.

Miss Evans led the way. The immaculate paths were made of slate stepping-stones and were edged with flowering borders. The paths were wide and smooth. There were no bumps to trip up unwary feet. The cottages were all on one level—no stairs to fall up or down. Knute wondered if his mother and father would like to live in such a place. Their small townhouse in Florida had a second story where the bedrooms were but they had never complained about it. Maybe they weren't old enough yet. He worried about them sometimes. There would come a day when they wouldn't be able to live alone . . . but maybe not. They were remarkable people and he hated to think of a time when they would be truly old . . .

The places weren't identical. Doors and window trim were different, but all were tasteful colors. Gardens were set in opposite directions and featured different plants. "Who takes care of the grounds?" Knute asked Fancy Evans.

"Oh, we have a full crew of gardeners," she answered. "But often the villagers themselves like to garden. We have 'best garden' contests in spring and fall and they're very popular affairs. Miss Ventress won last spring and Mr. Cullingham is famous for his roses." They were approaching his cottage. "He's planted them at the rear of his house near the patio. He says the sun is better for them there—something about morning versus afternoon sun. Push that button right there. Mr. Cullingham has a door chime that plays 'Anchors Aweigh'."

The man who answered the chime was tall and spare except for a little bulge above his beltline. His hair was pure silver, his eyes a bright hazel color, his skin tanned. He had smile lines, deep ones, around his eyes but after they told him the news he was certainly not smiling. "It's a terrible thing," he told Knute. "I can't imagine how she got herself locked in the larder. Roseanna had more sense than that."

Sitting in his well-appointed living room, Bill Cullingham explained that he and Roseanna were friends of long standing. "I met her some twenty-five years ago when I got out of the Navy and moved back to the city. Her husband Arnie belonged to the Boston Rotary Club and so did I. We became great chums, used to play bridge every week when my wife was still with us . . . How can I help you, Chief Severson? I don't quite understand why you're here although I suppose in a case of accidental death— It *is* accidental death, isn't it?"

Knute made a gesture that could mean anything but Cullingham seemed satisfied. Later, when he went over Officer Buono's verbatim notes, he read that Bill Cullingham hadn't seen Roseanna dela Mare since two nights previously, when he and Roseanna had played bridge with Ward Butler and Delilah Ventress. As for last night, he'd turned in about eleven-thirty ("Just after the news"), slept soundly ("I always do") and after breakfast mulched his rosebushes. He'd had breakfast in his own kitchen. He had been "thrown for a loop, I can tell you, at the news. I was really shocked. And what makes it even worse is that Gordon, her son, is out west somewhere, on vacation. Did you manage to reach him, Fancy? He was driving to Banff, I think. Roseanna said he wanted to get away from it all, although what 'it all' is I'm not sure. She'd set him up in the real estate business but I don't know how much real estate he ever sold . . ."

Ward Butler (full name Percival Edward Butler) had been located at the communal swimming pool doing one hundred laps. "Every morning, that's my routine. In summer I swim here, of course; in winter I drive over to the college. They have an indoor pool and since I'm an alumnus it's available. Babson, I mean." He snickered. "Not Wellesley."

He toweled his salt-and-pepper-colored head. "Damn fool thing for Roseanna to do, go into the cold room in the middle of the night. Raiding the icebox, I suppose. Don't know what she was after, ice cream maybe. Funny thing, I never cared much for sweets when I was younger but now I guess you could call me an ice cream–aholic . . ."

Ward Butler had a wife, Amanda, who was off with the majority of Shangri-la, sailing along Alaskan shores. "We never take vacations together," her husband confided. "We see enough of each other as it is." Percival Edward Butler, aged seventy-nine, retired attorney-at-law, was a big man with an incipient weight problem despite his daily swim.

And the last interview of the morning—Delilah Ventress, author, age . . . "I thought gentlemen never asked a lady's age." She'd twinkled at Knute. She was a small, cuddly-looking woman with a headful of curly, light brown hair. "Let's just say I'm old enough to be living here, is that sufficient?" It was sufficient, of course. Knute's interest in age was personal, he decided, the real question being: how did these people look and function so well at such advanced ages?

Delilah's story was much the same as Cullingham's and Butler's. She hadn't seen Roseanna since the bridge game. She was shocked beyond words, and tears came to her eyes when she learned of her death. She had astonishingly romantic eyes: "deep blue and dreamy" is what Officer Buono had written. She'd fondled Fifi, her equally curly haired French poodle, looked up and said, "You know, Chief Severson, I wouldn't be a bit surprised if someone put her in there and locked the door. It would be just the sort of thing that would happen to Roseanna."

Knute left his car in the driveway because the garage was occupied; Brenda's Dodge Aries took up one side, and on the other was Leif's 1973 Chevrolet, which showed some signs of the repairs he was making on it but still looked like a refugee from a junkyard. Leif was in Maine, where he was spending his first year as a counselor at summer camp. Knute wondered how he was doing.

He went in through the back door, smelled something cooking in the oven and peered inside. A casserole of some sort. He wasn't keen on casseroles. Roast beef would have been nice but they hadn't been eating as much beef lately. "Brenda! I'm home."

A muffled answer came from upstairs. Knute followed the sound. Brenda was in the middle of the bedroom floor, exercising to her Jane Fonda videotape. She was breathing hard and her face was shiny.

Knute made his way around her. "I thought this was your morning routine." He moved hangers, looking for his old jeans. The lawn needed mowing and since Leif was away . . .

"Didn't—have—time," panted Brenda while kicking her legs and waving her arms. She looked stuffed into her leotard, he thought en route to the bathroom. Probably it was an old one— too small. She'd gained weight in recent years. He hadn't. At least, not much. Maybe five pounds. Easy to take that off. Just go without bread and potatoes for a couple of days.

When he came out, the video was over and Brenda was lying

across the bed. "It's really better in the mornings," she said. "But I feel great after exercising. I really do."

"Good for you. Do I have time to mow the lawn?"

"The back part maybe. I'll be down as soon as I shower. There's a postcard from Leif on the kitchen counter by the telephone."

Printed on the postcard in block letters was WHY DIDN'T YOU TELL ME THAT KIDS ARE MONSTERS? I THINK I MAY SURVIVE BUT I'M NOT SURE I WANT TO. LOVE, LEIF. Knute chuckled and went out to mow the lawn.

Later, over gin and tonics, he told Brenda about Roseanna dela Mare and Shangri-la.

"No chance at all that it was an accident?"

"I don't see how. The Evans girl swears that the door handle was firmly closed when she opened it and it takes an extra push to set it right. And the loose light bulb, I don't like that at all . . . but I can't see any of those old-timers doing the deed. I wonder about motive and I wonder about agility. As far as motive is concerned, how do I know you don't lose your cool over a bridge loss at that age? I don't know what riles them. They live in a cotton-batting world over there. I'd vote right away for the son but it seems he's clear across the country. I'm anxious to talk to him."

"Any fingerprints on the light bulb? Or the door handle?"

"Not on the light bulb. The handle was smeared—Miss Evans' prints on the top. There should be somebody's prints on that light bulb. Somebody screwed the bulb into the fixture in the first place."

"But could fingerprints be wiped off without moving that cage contraption? Or could someone have moved it?"

"It's been up so long it's corroded. No one took it off. Maybe if you turned the bulb while holding a cloth against it . . . like this." He demonstrated in thin air. "What's for dinner?"

"Tuna casserole and a green salad. I've met Delilah Ventress, you know. Last year when we had the Wellesley authors tea at the library. A little thing with a curly wig?"

"Is it a wig? Yes, that's Delilah. She seemed like a nice little old lady. Very prim and proper."

Brenda laughed. "You should read some of her books. Very sexy."

"You read that stuff? I'm surprised."

"When something's on the bestseller list as long as some of her books are, you get curious. Besides, it's my duty as a library trustee—"

"Ho, ho, ho." Knute grinned.

"Well, I'll confess that I didn't hate the Ventress books. For the sort of thing they are, they aren't bad . . . Take that smug look off your face, Knute Severson, and let's go into dinner. I refuse to feel guilty over an occasional lowering of my reading standards. At least I don't keep *Playboy* in my night-table drawer."

"*Playboy*'s gotten very conservative." Knute swallowed the last of his drink. "They don't even have the centerfold anymore."

"The influence of the Hefner daughter, no doubt."

"Everything's changing," said Knute, pushing himself up from his chair. "It really surprises me, how much everything's changing."

Alice Buono operated the coffee urn at the police station. Knute had told her she wasn't obliged to act as cook and bottle washer but she'd said she didn't mind. "Besides, you guys make terrible coffee." She'd smiled, showing a left cheek dimple. When Knute had interviewed her prior to her appointment, he hadn't thought Alice Buono especially attractive. He'd decided, however, that she had the kind of looks that improved with time. Her hair was no special color. Brown, he thought, but on the light side. If he stretched a point he could say blond, ash blond, and her eyes were pale blue, almost turquoise. She was slim, maybe too thin, but he'd begun to appreciate thin. That was no doubt the influence of all this get-fit propaganda. When he'd been playing the dating game he'd been very interested in curves if he remembered correctly . . .

"Good morning, Chief." Here was Alice with the coffee. Knute reached for reports in his IN basket. He was not supposed to be caught daydreaming.

"Good morning, Officer Buono." The Officer Buono sounded awkward, he knew, but he couldn't bring himself to call her Buono as he called Beavers and Tracy and O'Malley and Pastori and the others by their last names. He didn't think Alice was quite right either. That sounded more like a secretary or even a maid and the lady was a police officer, by God . . .

"Gordon dela Mare is on his way back from Canada," she reported. "He left yesterday as soon as Miss Evans contacted him, and he plans to drive straight through from Banff, but even so I doubt if he'll get here before late tonight."

"I suppose it's too early for a report from Dr. Bell?"

"I'll give him a call if you want."

He shook his head. "I've learned that pushing the good doctor only slows him down. I'll be going out to Shangri-la later this morning. I'd like you to come along, so keep yourself available."

"Yes, sir."

He drank his coffee slowly, eyes still on the door where Alice had exited. She was twenty-four and lived with her mother. Her father was in some other state, maybe Vermont. He seemed to recall she'd told him Vermont. Her folks were divorced. Knute wondered how it would feel if his mother and father weren't still together. What did a man—or a woman—do when suddenly alone after years of marriage?

Lieutenant Pastori rapped and came in. "Here's the vacation duty roster." He handed over a set of calendar pages with names written in various dates. "I ran it through the computer. I think it works out that we're all covered."

"Thanks, Pastori. When are you going?"

"I'm going to wait until fall. I want to do some hunting. You're set for late August. Where are you taking the family?"

"I think we'll drive down to Florida. I haven't seen my folks in some time, and Leif and Brenda haven't seen them in two or three years. They aren't getting any younger, you know."

"Aren't we all," was Pastori's exit line.

Roseanna dela Mare's little house was decorated throughout in off-white, moss green and various shades of pink from hot to shell. The correct names were supplied by Officer Buono in her later written report.

Fancy Evans, looking very much like a California golden girl visiting Massachusetts, let them in and told them that Mr. Bancroft was returning from London. "He's very distressed but he assured me that it wasn't my fault." The former Mrs. Gordon dela Mare was motoring in from the Berkshires.

Knute informed her that Mr. dela Mare was also en route, expected late that night or maybe tomorrow morning.

"Oh, thank goodness. That does take some of the responsibility off me. Mr. Bancroft couldn't get a flight until tomorrow and I don't suppose Mrs. dela Mare has any real authority. There are funeral arrangements to be made and legal matters and the disposal of her lovely things . . ." She looked around. "I guess it's all right to let you go through them." Knute started to speak but she hurried on. "I mean, I know you must but I feel so . . . it's rather like prying, isn't it?" And she looked up at him with sad, wide blue eyes.

"We'll try not to disturb anything." Alice spoke quickly, woman to woman. "And it isn't prying, not really. It's looking for some sort of answer, some kind of message as to how this terrible thing happened. She'd want us to know."

"Yes." A tremulous smile came and went. "I guess she would. Then I'll leave it to you. I'll be in my office if you want me. You'll find the extension listed on the telephone."

"Nice going," said Knute to Alice.

"She's just nervous." Alice smiled at the compliment. "She's only a kid."

That made him grin but she either didn't see the grin or chose to ignore it. "Where shall we start?" she asked.

"The medicine cabinet."

In Roseanna's medicine cabinet they found Tylenol, Listerine, Bandaids, Preparation H, a prescription decongestant signed by a Dr. Guinness, over-the-counter allergy tablets, Alka-

Seltzer and another prescription from Dr. Guinness for Premarin. Knute didn't know what Premarin was but Alice did. "It's estrogen. Female hormones," she told him.

"I'm surprised at how little there is," said Knute. "I thought there'd be more. Dental adhesive and pills for constipation—stuff like that. All the TV ads show the elderly pushing that kind of thing."

"Maybe Mrs. dela Mare had her own teeth."

"At her age?"

"It does happen. My mother has all her own teeth."

"She's not in her late seventies, for God's sake."

"No. But I'll bet she has all her own teeth when she is. She takes good care of them."

The cosmetic collection was large. There were several kinds of creams and moisturizers. There were various shades of mascara and eye shadow and rouge and lipstick and powders and perfumes and colognes . . . "Eye oil," wondered Knute, putting the vial back in its place, "whatever that's for. She's spent a small fortune on these."

Alice nodded. "She's got all the best kinds."

From the bathroom they went into the kitchen. There they found an entire shelf of vitamins and vitamin supplements. One-A-Day vitamins, vitamins B, C, and D in separate containers, calcium with magnesium and zinc, lecithin . . . "What are all these supposed to do?" Knute asked.

"I don't really know. We'll have to ask. There's a health food store on Linden Street. I'll check into it when we get back. Just let me make a list."

In the refrigerator they found frozen Weight Watchers entrees; Stouffer's Light entrees; a bottle of red wine and a bottle of white wine, both opened and both imported. Also on the refrigerator shelves were a butter-margarine mixture, all the makings for salad, a container of buttermilk, four apples, three lemons and two leftover boiled potatoes.

They moved on to the living room, which featured an elegant secretary. The desk yielded a leather-bound, gilt-trimmed address book and a checkbook from a local bank in a matching case—the pale pink checks printed with background photos of gulls over a coral sea. Printed in the upper left-hand corner was "R. dela Mare, Alpha One, Shangri-la, Wellesley, MA 02181." A quick glance at the check stubs showed recent amounts paid to Filene's, Bonwit Teller and Ara's. Officer Buono, looking over Knute's shoulder, wondered what Mrs. dela Mare might have bought in a men's store like Ara's. Probably something for her son, she answered herself.

"Here's a letter from her son." Knute passed it along. "A bill from Dr. Guinness. That's a break. She'd seen her doctor recently; he'll know what her current state of health was. And here's a bunch of papers—what does this mean?" He read aloud, "At my age, you'd imagine memory would lose its sharpness but I have a headful of vivid pictures. It is possible that I've technicolored some to suit although even I can't be sure of that but what matter? I'll swear on a stack of Bibles that all I'll tell you is true and you won't care if it isn't because I've lived a fascinating life."

Knute riffled through the pages. There must have been fifty or more, carefully typed and double-spaced. "It looks like some sort of manuscript," he decided. His neighbor, Mercy Bird, was a writer and he'd seen her working with pages like that.

"Maybe she was writing her biography," Alice ventured.

"Autobiography," Knute corrected automatically. "Could be. I'll take it along so you can make copies, then we'll return it. There's the bookcase. What did the late lady like to read?"

The late lady liked to read novels, including those of Delilah Ventress. Most of the novels were straight off the bestseller list. She also enjoyed the Hollywood tell-all type of biographies and there were a dozen or more of these. A stack of magazines turned out to be copies of *Vogue, Town & Country* and *Vanity Fair.* A pile of papers was something called *W,* filled with colored photos of what they used to call the jet set.

A music center provided more catholic taste. The music of the forties was there—Glenn Miller, Benny Goodman and Artie Shaw—but so were Simon and Garfunkel, the Beatles, Willie Nelson with Julio Iglesias, Alabama and the Rolling Stones.

In the bedroom they found clothes: dresses and pantsuits and skirts and blouses and sweaters (in mothproofed cases) and many types of shoes—low heels, high heels, middle heels, boots, sandals, even a pair of running shoes.

"She wore a size seven," Alice noted, "and she had narrow feet. I think women's feet used to be smaller. My mother wears a six while I wear an eight. Lots of girls I know wear nines and tens."

"Does anything look odd to you? Out of place? Something that shouldn't be there?"

"Just the jogging shoes. You don't suppose she jogged, do you? At her age? And there's something missing."

"What's that?"

"Jewelry. You'd think that a woman like Mrs. dela Mare would have lots of jewelry. There isn't even a jewel box."

Knute grunted. "Good point. Maybe Miss Evans will have some answers. See if you can find something to put these papers in and we'll find out."

Fancy Evans did indeed have the answers to some questions. The villagers at Shangri-la had safe-deposit boxes in the administration building, where they kept their valuables. "I have the key in her bag, which I brought over here yesterday evening. I thought that was the wisest thing to do. I didn't do anything wrong, did I?" Knute refrained from snarling and simply shook his head. "I'm sure her jewelry will be in there. When her son gets here he can open it. You want to look through her handbag? Oh, gracious, of course. I didn't think of that. Wait here and I'll get it right away. I've got it locked in my desk drawer."

Roseanna's bag was of white straw. There'd been so many others in Roseanna's closet—bags matching shoes, bags of leather and silk and alligator and snakeskin—that he hadn't thought there'd be another. Inside it was a wallet made of very soft leather. Miss Evans said it was eel skin. It contained over a hundred dollars and some change, a driver's license, several credit cards including American Express and Visa, a book of stamps, a comb, four lipsticks, a compact with mirror, a Kleenex holder with tissues, several grocery coupons snipped from a newspaper ("Oh, we all save coupons," Fancy explained) and several sets of keys.

Fancy pointed out which keys were which. To the cottage, front and back doors; to the safe-deposit box; to the Center (yes, everybody had a key to the Center); luggage keys; car keys (Mrs. dela Mare drove a small Toyota); and a key Fancy wasn't sure about. Knute put everything back and handed the bag to her.

Dr. Guinness was the gynecologist who was on call for Shangri-la's ladies. Dr. Guinness' office was "just down the road, actually." Fancy recited the address and phone number while Alice wrote them down.

The pages that Knute thought might be a manuscript were just that. "Miss Ventress has been holding writing classes for anyone interested. Quite a few of the villagers signed up for them." Fancy Evans blushed. "I'm even trying my hand at it myself."

"So," said Knute later to Brenda, "I checked with Miss Ventress and she told me they were all taking the course: Evangeline Meeny, Ward Butler and Bill Cullingham as well as Fancy Evans and a bunch of the Alaska-trippers. It took some persuading but I managed to get copies of the priceless prose penned by Meeny, Butler and Cullingham. There might be something in those pages that could suggest a motive for murdering Mrs. dela Mare. Don't look at me like that! It's just a hunch. A hunch is something you go for when you haven't the least idea what to do next."

"Then she was murdered?"

"Dr. Bell, good old slow Joe, reports that he's been unable to find any trace of any suspicious substance to date. She'd dined on asparagus and shrimp and she'd had wine but not too much. The son is supposed to get back tonight. He'll be on my back tomorrow to release the body and we can't keep it forever, God knows. I asked about drugs and the answer is no. Not even aspirin in large amounts. But I know that woman didn't just walk into that freezer and close the door behind her."

"Maybe she did. Maybe she was despondent or had some horrible disease."

"Joe Bell didn't find any horrible disease."

"It could have been her mind."

"I'll find out more tonight. I've got an appointment with Dr. Guinness later this evening. What are we having for dinner?"

"Meat loaf. I've left it in the oven along with a potato. I've got to go out so I ate earlier."

"Out? Where?"

"A Library Trustees meeting." She picked up her purse and car keys.

"This early?"

"There's a sale at John Douglas. I thought I'd take a look in there first."

"Don't they close at six or five-thirty?"

"Not during sale days." She patted his cheek in passing. "See you later."

You'd think she'd manage to do her shopping in the daytime, thought Knute as he filled a plate and sat down to eat. He shuffled the papers he'd brought with him from Shangri-la and read as he ate.

Vangie Meeny's autobiography was handwritten with a leaky pen. It wasn't all that easy to read, especially since there were some misspellings. Knute made out:

My name is Evangeline Marie Meeny, born Dwyer, and I'm seventy-eight years old in this year of our Lord.

I've got a good son named Roger. Roger and his wife, Cecilia, have four sons: Kevin, Donald, Derek and James. They are my beautiful grandchildren.

Except for my spinal trouble my health is pretty good. I'm thankful for that.

My biggest disappointment in life is that John Wayne never got to be President of the United States. He would have been a wonderful President. He looked like a President: strong, tough, but kindhearted. He produced and directed *The Alamo;* you know, it was all about patriotism. I loved that picture. I loved all his pictures except those last ones where he played that old Rooster Cogburn. That wasn't my John Wayne at all.

Delilah Ventress says that the way to write a book is to write about somebody who's had lots of troubles. Then you give them some more troubles, pile it on. Then at the end the person with lots of troubles triumphs over all obstacles. That's me, you know. That's the story of my life.

The first obstacle in my life was . . .

The telephone rang. Knute groaned, pushed his hair back and went to answer it.

A man's voice asked, "Is Brenda there?"

"No, she's gone out to a library meeting. Who's this?"

"Ah, Chief Severson. This is Randolph Harper. I'm on the trustees board, too. I just wondered if she'd remembered. There are some reports I thought she might bring."

"Brenda seldom forgets anything like that."

"Yes, of course. It's just that I had an idea that one or two older ones might be helpful, but if she's gone, she's gone, so thanks very much."

"Can I do anything? If I can find them, I'll drop them off. I'm going out a little later."

"No, no, it's not that important. Just some figures on circulation from last year but we have the up-to-date ones. Thanks anyway; it's good of you to offer."

"It's no trouble. If I can find them—"

"I really don't want to put you out. Thanks again." The line went dead.

Just the same, he did look for the library circulation reports but he couldn't find what they wanted. By the time he'd finished looking it was pretty certain he'd be late. And of course he was.

The plaque beside the door read "V. S. Guinness, M.D." Knute rang the bell, heard a door close somewhere inside, then heard footsteps approaching. The footsteps were light and sounded young, sounded like . . .

High heels. The person who opened the door was a woman, slim, tall, sandy-haired, well dressed. "I have an appointment with Dr. Guinness," said Knute.

"You must be Chief Severson. Come in. I thought you might be wearing your uniform—you know, the one with all the gold braid that you wear in the Veterans Day parade."

He hated the uniform with the gold braid but the selectmen had hinted that they liked to see their chief in "a proper uniform." He'd demurred, said he preferred to march in his old uniform, but then Chairman of the Selectmen Georgia Pinson had told him that he "looked just like one of the rank and file" so gold braid it was. Especially after Selectman Ernie Kilmer had concurred, "Yes, by God, Chief, you do." He'd laughed his hearty laugh. "Dress it up a little, can't you? We can't tell the chief from the Indians." Ha, ha, ha. They'd all gotten a laugh out of that.

"Sit down, please." The lady had led him into a sitting room and motioned to a blue velvet armchair. "Now, what can I do for you? I presume it's about Mrs. dela Mare." She sat on a blue-striped sofa.

He shouldn't have been surprised. There were women bank presidents, engineers, architects, lawyers, women executives of all sorts these days. Why shouldn't Dr. Guinness, a gynecologist, be a woman? Women doctors were not rarities and never had been in his lifetime. Still, he hadn't expected it. Just one more of the little surprises he'd been experiencing of late. Unimportant surprises, but unsettling somehow. Just as though he weren't always in control.

"I'm sorry to be late," he began. "I got delayed on town business. Yes, I am here about Mrs. dela Mare. How was her health in general?"

"Quite good. Especially for her age." She picked up a folder from the coffee table in front of her. "I made copies of the pertinent tests for you. Blood pressure, acceptable; cholesterol, within reason; heart, lungs, liver, reproductive system, all as should be for a woman in her late seventies. I was truly surprised when I heard she'd died. That was before I knew the circumstances, of course." She looked directly at him and he noticed that her eyes were a rich, dark brown. "I rather find it hard to accept a verdict of accidental death, Chief Severson. That lady was in total control of herself, regardless of her age."

"How was her mental attitude?"

"Very positive. If you're considering suicide, you're way off base, in my opinion. Of course, I'm no psychiatrist, but . . . What does your medical examiner say?"

"The autopsy isn't complete yet. I take it that all the residents of Shangri-la have to be in pretty good physical shape. It's not a rest home, is it? They don't accept chronically ill patients, do they?"

"Not usually, no. Some of the residents have chronic ailments they've learned to live with."

"What happens if they do become seriously ill?"

"If we can cope with it in the patient's cottage, we do so. If she requires hospital care, I make the arrangements and oversee the treatment. As does Dr. Barton, the internist who deals with the male residents." She leaned back against the sofa pillows. "I cannot for the life of me understand why Mrs. dela Mare went into the refrigeration room. It's so unlike her! There are some of the ladies who can be a little—vague—at times. But not Roseanna."

"Somebody suggested the obvious—that she got hungry and was looking for something to eat. Like ice cream."

Dr. Guinness looked scornful. "Not Roseanna dela Mare. She

was into fitness, Chief Severson. She went faithfully to Gary
Tate's exercise classes, and she counted her calories."

"Gary Tate? Who's Gary Tate?"

"He's our physical fitness director. There's a complete spa at
Shangri-la. Gary was a onetime Mr. Massachusetts, or so I'm
told. Weight lifting. Muscle development. He's into all that. He
looks a bit like Michelangelo's *David* brought to life."

Knute shuddered inwardly at the thought. He closed his
notebook and got to his feet. "Thanks for seeing me. I hope I
haven't interrupted your evening."

"Doctors are used to interrupted evenings." She smiled.

"Yes, I guess they are. But thanks anyway." He was faintly
disappointed as he drove away. She might at least have offered
him a cup of coffee. It used to be that he never had an interview
with any young lady that didn't result in at least an offer of a
cup of coffee. How old was Dr. V. S. Guinness, anyway? In her
early thirties? He supposed that to her he looked like an old
man.

It was early yet so he drove to Shangri-la. Fancy Evans could
direct him to Gary Tate.

She was watching television in the lounge, a movie Knute
recalled seeing years before. "I'd like to talk to Gary Tate," he
told her. "Where can I find him?"

"He should be in his apartment above the gym." She turned
the TV off and looked at him with widened eyes. "Is it something about Roseanna? Of course it is. But Gary? You think
Gary . . ." Miss Evans held a potato chip bag that crackled as
she tightened her grasp on it.

"She took exercise classes from him, I understand. I need to
talk to everybody."

"Yes, of course. He should be there. Unless he's gone out.
Would you like me to call him?"

"If you would. Thanks."

She was gone longer than he expected so he turned the TV back on. Jack Lemmon and Tony Curtis were dressed up in women's clothes and carrying band instruments. While they stood beside a train Marilyn Monroe passed by. They stared after her. So did Knute.

"He's expecting you." Fancy Evans was back.

He wondered what else they'd talked about. "Thanks very much. I need to know where the gym is."

She told him. She looked a bit pale, almost distressed, he thought. Perhaps she had a thing for the muscle man. "It's just routine," he said, sounding like Jack Webb. She probably didn't know who Jack Webb was.

"I'm surprised to find you working so late." She had to raise her voice over the sound of the television.

"Well, there's a lot to do and the quicker the better."

"Yes, but . . ."

"But?"

"You're the chief. Don't you have people who do these things for you?"

"Sure. But I like to handle important matters myself."

"Important? Yes, I guess Mrs. dela Mare would be important. Do you"—she hesitated—"do you know how she died yet? I know she froze to death, but it seems to me that the question is why." And she looked at him with alarmed eyes.

"That's the question all right," said Knute.

Gary Tate was tall, golden, well muscled and well mustached. He was very gracious, excessively so.

"Come in, come in, what can I do for you, Chief Severson? I managed to get a parking ticket a couple of weeks ago but I paid that already and I don't imagine chiefs of police go around collecting parking ticket fines. Sit down, sit down. Can I get you a beer or something? Do you like Beck's? It's my favorite beer. You sit right here and I'll be right back." While he was in the kitchen Knute looked around.

Gary Tate was into bodybuilding, that was obvious, and several silver cups attested to the fact that he was good at it. The polished shine of the cups showed that he was proud of it too.

He was also into abstract art, it seemed. All four walls were hung with brilliantly colored canvases—deep reds, chrome yellows, inky blacks and deep purples. Knute couldn't tell whether they were any good but they certainly made "a statement."

The furniture was leather, chrome and glass. Naturally. A stereo component group and a television-VCR combination took up one wall, and a round table with two chairs another. The setup shouted young bachelor in the fast lane. Knute could imagine the little table set for two, the lights low, a fire in the Scandinavian-type fireplace, soft music on the stereo and a beautiful woman in the bedroom . . .

"Here you are. I don't know if you prefer a bottle or a glass so I brought a glass." Gary Tate offered glasses and bottles on a small tray.

"The bottle will be fine, thanks." He took a swallow. "I've come to ask you about Roseanna dela Mare."

Gary plopped into a leather chair and put his Adidas up on the matching ottoman. "I kinda thought that was the reason for the visit. I was really shook up when I heard what happened. She was something, that one. A remarkable woman."

"In what way?"

"She was a fighter. She wouldn't give in . . . age wasn't gonna slow Roseanna down. She was a woman who took care of herself, Roseanna was. She was on an exercise program that would have bushed a younger woman, but not her. That's 'cause she'd been exercising long before it became a big deal. She told me she'd exercised all her life. It showed. Well, you saw her. Didn't it show?"

"You aren't likely to look so good when you're dead." Knute spoke deliberately.

Gary looked abashed. "Well, take my word for it. She was in great shape. For her age."

"Nobody seems to know what she was doing in the freezer. It looks as though she went in there during the night. It's pretty hard to figure out why anybody would have gone to the Center in the middle of the night and walked into the freezer . . ."

That was the question: if there weren't any traces of drugs nor any signs of force, why would anybody go to the Center in the night and walk into the freezer . . . He realized he'd stopped talking and was asking these questions of himself. Rusty, that's what he was, not thinking as fast as he once had. In Wellesley there were very few serious crimes. Robberies in fancy houses, traffic accidents. He was out of practice, way out. Nothing like the old days of the Boston PD. God, that seemed another lifetime . . . the young Detective Third Grade Severson with his bachelor pad, his cat and his long list of eligible females . . .

". . . and she thought young," Tate was saying. "She was up on things, into what was happening. You read about people like Roseanna, way up there in years but real sharp. Like Katharine Hepburn, you know? She'd never let herself go, no way."

Knute tilted the beer bottle, pleased to find it was empty. "That's what everybody says." He got to his feet. "Well, I'll be going. Thanks for the beer. I'll get back to you if we need anything more."

"Sure. Anytime. Hey, do you know when the funeral is gonna be? I want to go."

"No, it's up to her son. He's due back anytime, I guess. The autopsy's over, so it's up to him."

"They did an autopsy?" Tate opened the door for Knute.

"Sure. It's standard operating procedure in cases like this."

"What did they find?" It was almost a throwaway question. Gary Tate was looking down, fiddling with the dead bolt on his doorjamb.

"Her heart stopped beating. That's what killed her."

"Heart?" He looked up quickly, a question in his eyes.

Knute nodded.

Tate sighed. "I guess you never know when you reach a certain age. Something's got to give."

No, thought Knute, going out to his car, you never know. He hadn't lied when he'd told Gary Tate that Roseanna's heart had caused her death. After all, that's the way we all go. Our hearts stop beating.

The clock in his car told Knute that it was half past eleven. He swung by the library on his way home to see if the meeting was over. The place was dark.

But Brenda wasn't home yet. He left the door unlocked for her and got ready for bed. While he was brushing his teeth he heard her come in. "Where have you been?" he asked when she came into the bedroom.

She raised her eyebrows. "You know where I've been. The Library Trustees meeting."

"The place was as dark as a tomb when I went by half an hour ago."

He could almost see her hackles rise. "What does that mean? When you went by? You're checking up on me these days?"

He shrugged. "Just happened to pass by on my way home. Sorry."

"We went out for coffee afterward. That's where I've been. At Mr. Donut on the Pike. Want to check it out?" There were red spots on her cheeks, and her eyes flashed.

"Don't be a dope," said Knute and slid into bed.

Brenda was outside when Knute came downstairs the next morning. He had time for coffee, but that was about all.

"I moved my car to the street so you could get yours out," Brenda said when she came in. "What are you reading?" She was wearing shorts and a T-shirt and her hair was pulled back in a ponytail. Old trying to look young? Knute wondered.

Knute told her about the Shangri-la writing class and moved the file in her direction. He took another swallow of coffee and went on with the pages marked Bill Cullingham:

Often on Saturday nights I would accompany my mother and father who would take my grandmother and grandfather shopping. I was seven on one such Saturday night in the spring of 1920. My grandfather said that he wasn't feeling too well but he'd go along anyway.

Those days there were no shopping malls so Saturday night was THE night everybody went to town. My mother and father went off to shop, leaving me sitting in the back seat with my grandmother. My grandfather was sitting in the passenger side of the front seat. We were parked in front of Dolan's drugstore on Main Street. Suddenly my grandfather coughed. He coughed again and his head tipped backward, then dropped forward onto his chest.

My grandmother leaned forward and put her hand on his shoulder. She asked, "Are you all right, Jimmy?" He didn't answer.

Just then my father arrived. Sensing the situation, he went into Dolan's for help and a couple of fellows came out and helped my father carry my grandfather into the drugstore, where the pharmacist tried to revive him. My mother eventually arrived, a doctor was summoned, and we all stood around waiting until my mother finally told me that Gramp was dead.

My mother and I stayed with my grandmother for a few days. During the middle of the following week I came down an open staircase at my grandmother's that ran parallel with the small living room. I looked down and saw a coffin with a dead man in it. An open coffin with a dead man in it wearing my grandfather's clothes.

"Want some more coffee?" asked Brenda. He nodded, his mind on what he was reading. Cullingham had skipped a few years.

It was my first trip on a merchant ship. I signed aboard at Newport News, Virginia, on February 6, 1942. It was an old Standard Oil tanker called the *Chester O. Swain* and it was already loading fuel. We sailed two days later, heading south along the coast. There were a couple of ships ahead of us and a few more astern of us spaced a couple of miles apart. We had an armed guard Navy gun crew to man a five-inch gun mounted aft and two .50 caliber machine guns. We had no escorts of any kind for protection from German U-boats that had been making their presence felt all down the East Coast.

A particularly dangerous place was Diamond Shoal near Cape Hatteras, where subs would wait for passing ships. I was a lookout on the twelve-to-four midwatch. The second morning out I was awakened by a terrific explosion. I sat up in my bunk and shouted at Ellison in the bunk across from me, "Torpedo!" I pulled on my dungarees and headed topside. Everything was calm as I ran through the crew's mess quarters. A couple of guys were playing cards. It turned out that the Navy gun crew was simply testing the five-inch gun.

That night a tanker about ten miles astern of us was hit. We could see she was burning but really never heard another thing about her. Without further incident we arrived in Baytown, Texas, where we were to take on another cargo of oil.

My shipmate Wally and I decided to sign off the ship. We weren't sure what it was we had in mind. We were paid off with a little more than a week's pay, which in those days wasn't much, and took a bus to New Orleans. We stayed in some third-rate motel and next morning headed for the shipping offices to see if we could find another ship to sign on. We had about twenty bucks apiece so we didn't have much choice.

On Canal Street we ran into an old pal who had been in our section at maritime school in St. Petersburg. He told us he was signed aboard a new oil tanker that was taking on a load of bunker fuel at the Atlantic Refinery up in Baton Rouge. He said they had openings for a few seamen and also some wipers for the engine room. He was staying in town for the day but suggested we hop right up there. So we went to Baton Rouge.

We signed aboard. She was the *E. J. Henry* but no one knew where the ship was headed. We sailed the next night just after dark down the Mississippi. The next day we were in the Gulf, heading south.

The next port we saw was Colón, at the entrance to the Panama Canal. So now we knew where we were headed: the Pacific. Next day found us going through the locks, just like going up a gradual flight of stairs. I was assigned the job of oiling the cable foremast stays. I sat in a boatswain chair that was shackled onto the stay and was then pulled up to the top of the mast by a rope secured to the shackle. The rope was woven through a block at the top of the mast, then back down to a winch on the deck. I smelled of oil and fish tar for two days.

When we got out into the Pacific, a couple of days later, we were told our destination was Sydney, Australia. It was in this ocean and on this trip that I experienced the worst storm I've ever been in. The wind blew between gale and hurricane force for almost three days. The seas were mountainous. I shared quartermaster lookout duties. The second night, I was on the wheel when the captain, an old Norwegian, said to the second mate, "We've got to come about and get this sea on our stern or we'll break in two." We were a big tanker for those days, over five hundred feet. The thought of coming about in those seas . . . I couldn't imagine it.

The skipper commanded, "Five left rudder." It took about twenty seconds before the bow started falling off to port, then he shouted, "Ten left rudder." When we got into the trough, parallel with the waves, it was really scary. We started to roll slowly, and with each roll we tipped farther, mostly to port, until one time we rolled so far I was sure we were going to capsize. We just hung.

At last, slowly, the ship righted itself. We had managed to turn the corner and with the sea hitting us more and more on the stern we steadied.

We ran with the sea behind us for over twelve hours. Then the seas subsided and the evening became calm so we headed again for the southwest. Our orders had been changed; we were to go now to Fiji. We finally arrived in Suva. It was hot. We unloaded half our cargo into shore tanks.

We were then ordered to proceed to Nouméa, New Caledonia, and told that upon leaving Suva we would pick up our destroyer escort. A ship appeared on the horizon on our starboard beam when we were just an hour out. At first we were worried because we thought she might be Japanese but as she moved closer to us she was identified as DD368, USS *Flusser,* our escort to Nouméa.

There we transferred the rest of our cargo to a rusty British tanker. We traded our cigarettes for their beer. Everybody was happy.

Our trip back to the States was uneventful. We landed in San Pedro, where Wally and I paid off. We went up to L.A. for a couple of days and then took the train for New York. I thought maybe I ought to join the Navy. Wally thought he should, too.

"Your coffee's getting cold," said Brenda.

Knute took a sip. It was cold so he pushed it aside and refused another. He found his place and continued to read.

We were at Okinawa the day the war ended with Japan. The next morning our ship was sent to Sasebo, a port that Allied ships hadn't entered since before 1941. It was located on the southern island of Kyūshū. We steamed into a carefully concealed harbor and made for a dock near the middle of town. I couldn't imagine where everyone was—it was like a deserted city. We had to jump on the dock and handle our own mooring lines. I walked onto the dock, looked up and down and saw nothing but rows of Quonset-type buildings. And then I thought I saw a head jut out from around the corner of one of those buildings.

I just stood there and tried to look pleasant. At last a little Japanese boy about twelve years old had the courage to come up to me. I gave him a Hershey bar and then I had lots of company. About twenty kids showed up from nowhere.

Now I think I'd better tell about Nagasaki—

"Knute, aren't you going to be late?" Brenda couldn't have interrupted at a more interesting place.

"What's the point of being chief if you can't be late? Yes, I've got to go. I'll get back to this later."

Brenda picked up a sheaf of papers clipped together. "This seems to be by R. dela Mare. Is it fact or fiction? What do you expect to get out of this, anyway?"

Knute shrugged. "Background. Maybe a motive. I'm out in left field so far. On the surface those people at Shangri-la could be characters in a come-share-our-lifestyle video. They've lived a lot of years. Maybe there's something in these ramblings that will give me a handle on the reason for Roseanna's death."

"What about the usual reasons? Money? Passion? You've counted them out?"

"I don't know yet about money. I'll see the son today. But passion? At their age? How about revenge? Some of these old-timers get senile, you know. Can take offense at almost anything. Want to do me a favor if you've got time?"

She smiled wryly. "I may have to consult my busy schedule. What do you want me to do?"

"Read some of those things and make notes. I'd like your opinion. Anything that strikes you as interesting, pertinent, out of the ordinary. You know." He patted her hair. "I've got to go. See you later."

"Ummm," said Brenda. When he backed his car out of the driveway he could see her through the kitchen window. She was reading. She was reading Roseanna's story.

At my age, you'd imagine memory would lose its sharpness but I have a headful of vivid pictures. It is possible that I've technicolored some to suit although even I can't be sure of that but what matter? I'll swear on a stack of Bibles that all I'll tell you is true and you won't care if it isn't because I've lived a fascinating life.

I was born in a root cellar in the midst of a cyclone. I'm told the cyclone was ferocious and the root cellar crowded. My mother was there, of course, and her mother and her mother's mother and my mother's sisters, Jessie and Bedelia. You will immediately observe that there were no men present. There were various reasons for this but the main one was that the women in our family always outlived the men; thus my great-grandmother, my grandmother and even my mother were widowed.

The year was 1910 and my father was, so I am told, an adventurous sort, who managed to get himself killed at the age of twenty-four. He did it the hard way, by drowning. I say the hard way because our only body of water deep enough for that purpose was the somewhat sluggish Arkansas River. They said he fell in and, being unable to swim, lost his life. It happened, they said, during a Sons of the Pioneers picnic.

I've seen pictures of my family, photographs taken about that time; therefore I can envision the scene of my birth.

My mother, Dulcie, sweat-soaked, frightened, her large, round brown eyes more used to laughing but now opened wide in terror, her thick, brown braid lying across one shoulder, straining to give birth, thinking dear God, let it be over.

Her sister Jessie, reddish-golden curls piled high and falling low, amber eyes avid, abhorring the scene but loving the excitement. Bedelia, the blonde, wide eyes gray-green, skin paler than the others', trying to help but awkward. "Put the lantern down, Bedelia, before you drop it."

And then there was Grandmother Lily. Big-boned, gray-haired, eyes as blue as the sky. My great-grandmother, Evelyn, the small one. We got progressively taller through the generations but the little, silver-haired, birdlike lady could lay you low with a word. Her eyes were like icicles and she preferred to be called by her first name.

The women of the Staley family squatted in a root cellar beneath the fury of a Kansas cyclone and welcomed me into the world. The world of Kansas, that is, in 1910.

They named me Roseanna.

Our house was large and well furnished. By that I mean I can recall crawling, then toddling, then walking, then running through many rooms filled with many things. Golden oak tables and chairs, leather lounges and carved bureaus, brass beds, rose-patterned carpets, lace curtains. Crystal vases and gilded mirrors, even an organ. The organ came from Sears, Roebuck and Company. It was a marvelous, monstrous piece of furniture with broad pedals at its foot, pedals I learned to push down when I learned to crawl. Only Aunt Jessie could play the beast and she would oblige only when she was so inclined. Aunt Jessie didn't do anything she didn't want to do. I learned that at an early age. Maybe that's why I followed her around. She was different from Mother and Bedelia. I thought she was beautiful. When she was out I was often in her bedroom, fascinated by such mysterious items as cold cream, perfumes and curling irons, to say nothing of Dr. Worden's Female Pills and La Dores Bust Food.

Aunt Jessie worked as a bookkeeper for the Boston Store, our largest and best emporium. She was the middle daughter (Mother being the eldest and Bedelia the youngest) and declared she intended to be a spinster. "I am not the type to kowtow to some boring male," she would often say.

Dulcie Randolph, nee Staley, was the stay-at-home. She looked after me, did the cooking, the cleaning, the starching of curtains and even the beating of rugs.

Aunt Bedelia was a teller in a bank. Grandmother worked in the sausage room in one of the meat-packing houses. She stuffed sausages into gut casings. We never served sausages in our house.

Great-grandmother Evelyn was an excellent seamstress. Armed with the necessary needles, pins, threads, sharp shears, trimmings, tailor's chalk, et cetera, she would sometimes spend days at the home of a wealthy patroness creating Eton suits, evening gowns, indoor dresses and traveling costumes. She even made trousseaus with delicate handworked lingerie and bridal creations adorned with ribbons, bows, seed pearls, flounces, lace and silk flowers. When I slipped unseen into Great-grandmother Evelyn's room I went because I wanted to walk in too-big satin slippers, to wear too-long gloves on my small hands and perhaps an egret plume in my tangled hair. Roseanna, two years old and yearning to be a swan.

The house we lived in in Kansas was a two-story, white clapboard house with a wide porch across the front and a small porch running off the back door. My bedroom was over the kitchen, looking out on the roof of the porch above that back door. Some nights in summer when it got real hot I took my pillow and sheet out on the roof for sleeping. It was lovely to look up and see the stars.

Out in the back of the house was a barn and the famous root cellar "where Roseanna was born." Also there was a windmill that brought water up from a well.

In the barn we kept a buggy and Brown Betty, our horse. Grandmother Lily and Aunt Bedelia walked to work but Aunt Jessie needed transportation so she took the horse and buggy. When Great-grandmother Evelyn needed to visit a client they either sent for her in their rig or automobile, or Aunt Jessie dropped her off on her way to work. Aunt Jessie was quite good at driving the horse and buggy. Mother was quite good at caring for Brown Betty—feeding, watering and currying—but she was afraid to drive her, especially since there were getting to be so many automobiles on the streets.

I walked to school. I would have walked to school no matter how far (and it was quite a ways) because everybody walked to school.

Near our house was Hildebrand's General Store and Grogan's Drug Store. We had a branch post office not far away, near the packing house where Lily worked. Also in that neighborhood was a grain elevator where the farmers brought their wheat; Bedelia's bank; and a restaurant called the Stockyards Café. We had just about everything we needed within walking distance in our part of town.

Still, it was exciting to go downtown with Aunt Jessie. She'd take me with her when I needed new shoes because she got a discount from the Boston Store and because, as she said, they carried "quality merchandise," so why not have the best?

In addition to the Boston Store, downtown meant shop after shop offering all manner of things, plus several cafés, including a Chinese restaurant and a cafeteria named Wolfe's where Aunt

Jessie would sometimes take me for lunch. I always had the same thing: chicken soup and mashed potatoes with butter in the middle.

The rest of the day downtown I would spend waiting for Aunt Jessie to get through with work. I spent it at the public library. Once inside the library I didn't care if she ever came.

Not that it was boring at the Boston Store. Aunt Jessie would leave Brown Betty and the buggy at the livery stable and, taking me by the hand, lead me into her place of business. I can see it now—a long building with a mezzanine at the back and stairs leading up. The walls were lined with shelves and in the middle were more shelves back to back, with tables in between. All sorts of wonderful things were displayed on these counters and tables and shelves. Twenty salespeople worked in the Boston Store, making it an emporium, Aunt Jessie told me. Running along the ceiling were trolley lines holding wire baskets. When someone bought something the clerk would make out a sales slip, take the money from the customer, put both in one of these wire baskets and pull a cord that sent the basket and contents up to Aunt Jessie's office in the mezzanine, where change was made. Then she'd pull another cord and send it zinging back down in that same basket.

I was going through some old souvenirs a while back and found an advertisement from the Boston Store. The date was torn off but it must have been around the time I was born. A lady's tailor-made suit cost $10. Shoes were $1.50. A gentleman's fancy suit went for $9. A 42-piece dinner set could be had for $2.95, and a sewing machine for $12. Quite a difference from today, yes, but my Aunt Jessie, who had a very good job, made $10 for a six-day week, working eight to six-thirty with half an hour for lunch. Still, we did all right. With four of us working, we had most things we wanted. I never felt poor.

Great-grandmother Evelyn owned our house and made many of our clothes; we had our transportation and it didn't cost much to feed Brown Betty; and Grandmother could buy meat cheaply from her place of business. We were pretty well off. I expected it would be that way forever. Everyone worked to make things come out right and then it went on just like that. They lived happily ever after.

The first time I ever remember waking up worried was when Mrs. Cudahy brought Great-grandmother Evelyn home in the middle of the afternoon. She'd taken sick, Mrs. Cudahy explained, keeled right over in the midst of a fitting, and we thought maybe we'd better call the doctor.

"I'm all right," Evelyn protested. "I just got a little light-headed. It's the heat."

It sure was hot. My dress and bloomers were sticking to me. Mother took Evelyn upstairs and told her to get out of her corset and into a wrapper; then she'd bring her a cold cloth and some lemonade. No, Evelyn didn't want any lemonade but the cold cloth sounded good . . . Well, now, I thought, she'll be all right, and I went out to play. But she didn't come down to supper that night and the next morning I woke up worried.

Now I know what was wrong.

Now we call it cancer of the colon.

Then we didn't call it anything but we knew it was something awful.

Mother gave the best of care to Evelyn. I didn't get to see Great-grandmother very often because she was usually "sleeping," Mother would tell me.

The only good thing about it was that she didn't last long. Just a little over three months. Since we weren't truly religious and our house wasn't that big we had the funeral at Walker's Funeral Home.

I have two distinct memories of Evelyn's funeral. Mr. Walker, who greeted everyone at the door, combed his hair sideways instead of front to back. And afterward, at the cemetery, all the flowers were tied with gorgeous wide satin ribbons in pastel colors. Somebody, Bedelia I think, went back when it was all over and picked up all the ribbons and brought them back to me. I used them for ballet costumes with my white petticoat when I played toe dancer in the old pink toe shoes Jessie used to wear when she was young and took lessons in aesthetic dancing.

It wasn't long after Great-grandmother Evelyn passed on that we acquired a roomer. It was decided in a family discussion that we could use the money we would get by letting Evelyn's room. It was decided also that our roomer (not our boarder, just roomer) would have to be a gentleman roomer (women are too fussy and besides, they're usually home all day) who did not drink or smoke.

Aunt Jessie put up a notice at the Boston Store; Bedelia did the same at her bank; Lily put one up at her packing house; and Mother posted a small card at Hildebrand's General Store. I never did find out where he came from—from which notice, I mean—but the result was Victor.

Brenda marked her stopping place. She wrote a note and clipped it to the first page.

She was in her late seventies when she died. Her writing sounds as though she planned an autobiography in detail. A very determined young girl emerges and I presume she ended up as a very determined old lady. Actually, I'd like to read more. Do you suppose there are any more pages around?

I don't really see that this is going to help you, Knute. I don't mean it's a waste of time exactly but I read this one as well as

Bill Cullingham's, where only one page tells about family life. Then he jumps to his adventures in World War II. Hers is all about family; his has very little about family. Does that mean anything? I suppose so.

I think you need a psychiatrist to look these things over if you feel they're that important. I won't have any more time today— I didn't get a chance to tell you but I'm going into Boston today. The trustees have been invited to lunch followed by a tour of the Boston University libraries. I should be home in time for dinner. If not, I'll call . . .

Gordon dela Mare was waiting for Knute at the station. He was tall and somewhat overweight, with dark hair and pale eyes. There was a slight resemblance to Roseanna—only slight, Knute thought. He guessed his age to be around his own, or maybe a little younger. Knute liked to pick out something unusual about everyone—that way he could better remember them—but he couldn't attribute anything special to Gordon dela Mare.

"What have you found out?" he wanted to know. "How did my mother die?"

Knute apologized for keeping him waiting. "Would you like some coffee? I understand you've been driving all day and all night."

"Thanks." Dela Mare's voice was little more than a murmur. He sounded exhausted, which wasn't surprising after a two-thousand-mile drive. When Alice Buono brought in the coffee he stirred himself to ask, "Got any sugar substitute? I'm on a diet." He smiled wryly. "I'm always on a diet."

"I'm afraid I don't have much to report to you," Knute began.

Dela Mare waved a plump hand. "If you don't know anything new, don't bother. The Evans girl filled me in on the situation to date. I've got to see the funeral director so we can get everything squared away. Then I'd like to sleep for about a month. After that it may begin to make sense to me—but I doubt it."

He drank from his coffee mug and made a face. "I've had so

much coffee in the last twenty-four hours I'm awash. Is it okay to take the body? Can I call the funeral home?"

"I'll make sure." Knute got Dr. Bell's office on the telephone. He was told the medical report was on its way to him, and that the body could indeed be released.

When Knute hung up and looked back, Gordon dela Mare's eyes were closed. The man was really beat. "Mr. dela Mare?"

"Uhm? Yes?" The eyes opened. There were dark circles beneath them.

"I think you'd better hit the sack—you're out on your feet. The body can be released. If you'll tell me who you want to handle it I'll call them and have them pick it up. You can go along later."

Gordon blinked. "Fine. That would be fine. Waterman's, I guess. Yes, Waterman's would be fine. Tell them I'll come by later today."

"I'll tell them you'll come by in the morning. You're not in any special rush?"

"No. No. No rush. There's people I have to notify . . ."

"Maybe Mrs. dela Mare can help with that."

"Mrs. dela Mare? You mean Catlin? Don't tell me *she's* here."

"Yes, she's here with your daughter. They came yesterday as soon as they heard. I don't know where they're staying but Miss Evans should have that . . ."

Dela Mare put his elbow on the desk. He propped his head in his hand, nearly knocking over the coffee mug. "The vultures are gathering in the trees," he said.

"You think you can get home all right? How far do you have to go?"

"I live in Lincoln but I've taken a room at the Inn." He pushed himself up.

"I'll have somebody drive you."

"No, I'm okay." He headed for the door and collided with the doorjamb.

Knute punched the intercom. "Tracy? Are you there? Tracy, drive Mr. dela Mare to the Treadway Inn. Make sure he gets into his room. He's really bushed."

He watched them go off. Was this more than just fatigue? No way to be sure without a checkup, and no time for that now. Besides, he had no legal right to do a blood test for drugs or alcohol on Gordon dela Mare—he wasn't a murder suspect. He'd been two thousand miles away.

Hadn't he?

Lieutenant Beavers brought reports into the office: Alice Buono's neatly typed condensation of yesterday's investigations, as well as Beavers' interviews with the kitchen employees and Shangri-la security chief. Dr. Bell's medical report was among them. Lieutenant Beavers waited while Knute read, ready to answer questions.

Knute scanned, then looked up at Beavers. "Nothing plus nothing totals zero. They saw no evil, heard no evil and therefore speak no evil. Which leaves us with one unexplained corpse."

Lieutenant Beavers rubbed his hand over his crew-cut. Crew haircuts, thought Knute, are they coming back? "The security guards patrol in a Jeep. Unless somebody was making a racket it would be pretty easy to move around that place at night, especially if you belonged there. They're on skeleton staff, too; half of them are off on vacation."

Knute referred to the report. "Harold Murphy, age fifty-eight; Leonard Baines, age sixty-two. They're getting along in years, aren't they?"

"Oh, they're gung ho enough, I guess. They were a little bit hostile, to be honest with you. I guess they got the idea we were blaming them, so they came on tough to me. Said they knew their business. Said the job was a piece of cake anyway. Said everybody went to bed by ten o'clock and the bad news was boredom. Said nobody was wandering around Shangri-la that night."

Knute sighed. "Somebody was. I've got to go out there again this morning. I'll start from the beginning one more time. I'll take Officer Buono; she's a better typist than you are." He grinned at Beavers. "Anything else on your mind? Anything come up while I had my head in the sand?"

Beavers indicated the rest of the reports. "Nothing serious. Some vandalism at the high school. I guess, now that school's out, the little SOBs got nothing else to do. A fender bender on Route 9, no injuries. A pretty quiet night altogether."

"Lots of people out of town." Knute shuffled the papers together and left them in his IN basket. He intended to go over them again. "The Cape gets it this time of year."

"It couldn't happen to a nicer place," said Beavers on his way out.

Robert Bancroft, ensconced behind his desk, reminded Knute of Arnold Schwarzenegger: both were big, fair-complexioned, brown-haired, bony-faced guys with efficient-looking teeth. Fancy Evans had filled him in on recent events on the ride out from the airport, Bancroft said. He patted her shoulder in an avuncular way. Seated beside him, notepad at the ready, she gazed at him with puppy eyes.

"Miss Evans has been very helpful," Knute told him.

"Yes, of course. She always is. There will be an inquest, I gather. I'll wager that I can predict the results. Death by misadventure. Isn't that the term for accidental death?"

Knute allowed that that was a possibility. "Miss Evans, you

told us how you opened the door to the freezer, but I don't recall why you went to the freezer in the first place. That isn't your normal territory, is it? I should think Lulu Greer or one of her helpers would have been the one to open the door and find the body."

Fancy Evans flushed. "I went to get my fertility figure. My Haitian carving. You didn't notice it? Probably not—it was in a carton. It's about this high"—she indicated its height with her hands—"a carving of a woman. Primitive, but very well done. I bought it at an auction and the man sitting next to me said that sometimes those things from the tropics have termites." She was explaining to Robert Bancroft now. "And I said, 'Oh, good heavens, what shall I do?' He told me to freeze it for a couple of days. If there were any bugs in it, that would kill them. I knew it was too big to go in my refrigerator . . . and then I remembered the freezer and that's where I put it last weekend. I figured I'd give it plenty of time . . . I hope I didn't do anything you wouldn't approve of?"

Robert gave her shoulder another pat. "Of course not."

Knute glanced at Alice Buono, who caught his eye and gave a tiny shrug. He informed Bancroft and Miss Evans of Gordon dela Mare's whereabouts and announced his plans to further interview the villagers in residence.

Bancroft looked pained. "I trust you're being diplomatic. They aren't as resilient as they seem to be, you know."

"We're wearing kid gloves." Knute nodded to Alice, a signal to go.

"Strange expression, that," said Bancroft.

"What?"

"Handling with kid gloves. I haven't seen kid gloves in years but as I recall, the softness was felt in the wearing, not in the touching."

"Hmm. Yes. I'm sure you're right." Knute looked at Alice again—this time she merely blinked. "We're being, as you said, diplomatic."

"He sounds British," said Officer Buono as they made their way to Delilah Ventress' cottage.

"He sounds on the gay side to me." Knute couldn't put his finger on the reason Bancroft rubbed him the wrong way.

"Oh, I don't think so." Alice sounded quite positive.

"Yeah? How can you be so sure?"

"Fancy Evans doesn't think so. And she would know."

"Thank you for bringing back the papers." Miss Ventress held her barking poodle so Knute could put the papers of the "class autobiographies" on a foyer table.

"Quiet, Fifi," Miss Ventress spoke sternly and the dog wagged its tail. "She'll stop in a minute. She thinks it's her duty. Did you want to talk to me? Let's go into the living room where we can be comfortable and where I've left a box of doggie biscuits one of which will help insure silence. Won't you sit down, Chief Severson, Officer—Buono, is it?"

"You have a good memory." Alice smiled and her dimple came and went.

"Oh, I have to in my business. In writing, you see, you deal with a great many characters and if you call someone Mary in the first chapter and Jane in the tenth you've made a serious gaffe. I suppose you'd like to know what I know about Roseanna. I can begin by telling you that I felt sorry for her."

"Sorry?"

"Yes. Underneath that 'queen of the hive' exterior she was really a tragic person. She lost everyone she ever cared for, isn't that sad? Her entire family when she was young, and then later her husband, and even her son—although in a different way . . ."

"Her entire family? How did she lose her entire family?"

"Surely you must have read about it—no, you're too young. It was at a family outing, a summer picnic. Somehow poison got into the food, the potato salad I think, although it could have been the lemonade—anyway, they died. Her mother, her aunts, her grandmother, her stepfather, her uncle by marriage, all of them. A terrible terrible thing for anyone, but especially so for a young girl."

"Where was she?"

"She had eloped with a young baseball player that very day. That was what saved her."

"Why isn't all this in her papers . . . ?"

"Oh, she hadn't gotten to that part yet. Telling such a tale can be therapeutic but it's not easy to put it down. She was working toward it; that's one reason she was taking my course, you see. I told her it would be good for her. It would help her to sleep at night—"

"She had trouble sleeping? It wouldn't have been odd for her to be roaming about at night?"

"Oh, no. She tried all sorts of remedies. She exercised so that she would be weary and she was very careful about what she ate (certain foods can keep you awake, you know)."

"There weren't any sleeping pills in her medicine cabinet," observed Officer Buono.

"Oh, my, no. She wouldn't take those. Considered them dangerous. She'd say, 'Look what happened to Marilyn Monroe. And to my husband.' He died of a sleeping pill overdose, you know."

"No, I didn't know."

"I think it would be very helpful if you did a little research at the library, Chief Severson. I'll make a note of the dates and you can look them up in the file copies of old newspapers. It's all on microfilm now, of course. In the old days I used to love the feel and the smell of old newspapers. Writers have to do a great deal of research, you know. Historical romances must be factually accurate, then one can let one's imagination run riot . . ."

"Tell me about you, Miss Ventress. Have you ever married? Do you have children, relatives?"

"I'm quite alone, Chief Severson. Except for Fifi, of course. My parents are long gone and my only brother died when I was young. I never married. I think it's because I'm too romantic. As far as I can see it isn't true that people live happily ever after."

"I get the impression that you knew Mrs. dela Mare in her youth."

"Oh, yes. We attended high school together. We weren't intimates but we knew each other. In those days one knew everyone, it seemed. Of course there were fewer people. And we didn't jump about so much—the auto was fairly new and roads were hardly highways." She smiled apologetically. "That meant we were terribly insular, I'm afraid. And naive. Can't you sense that in the stories they're writing? Roseanna's detailed description of *things*—things were very important to her; Bill's concentration on the war he fought in, his biggest adventure; Ward's acerbic attitude toward women; Vangie's self-congratulatory tone . . ." Another smile. "Actually, this writing class is giving me birth pains. I'm getting all sorts of ideas for a new novel set in the early years of the twentieth century. They'll all be characters in it though I'll never let them know it," she chuckled like a child playing witch.

"Are you telling me that you all knew each other before coming here?"

"Of course. We're all more or less the same age, why wouldn't we?"

Knute blamed himself for not reading all those pages. He'd only scanned a few. Longtime associations could breed old grudges . . . "I'm surprised that you've all ended up in the same place. That's unusual, wouldn't you say?"

She shook her honey-colored curls. "Oh, I don't think so. Quite the contrary given the fact that we all gravitated toward the East Coast—to Boston, the only really nice city on the Atlantic. Shangri-la is the only place of its kind around here. It's the new trend, you know. If you have the assets you invest them in living quarters. It may seem strange to you because you're still a young man, Chief Severson, but when one gets older life gets even more precious. When one is young, dying is only a word, but when you pass a certain age it becomes an eventuality. The only question is when? The answer is not now. Ten years from now, maybe. Or next year. Next month. Next week. Tomorrow. Never now."

Back in the car, Knute got behind the wheel. He'd turned down Officer Buono's offer to drive. Being chauffeured by a woman? What would that look like?

"I'm trying to get age into perspective." Buono looked pensive. "My mother is forty-six." Knute winced inwardly. "My grandmother is in her early sixties. I thought my mother was old, kind of, and my grandmother really old. But I guess they aren't. I mean, my mother certainly isn't." Thanks alot, thought Knute. "And my grandmother is younger than Miss Ventress and the others." She turned to Knute. "I wonder, what is old?"

"Beats me."

Officer Buono looked out and saw the Shangri-la gates. "Aren't we going to Mr. Cullingham's?"

"Later. I've got to get caught up with my homework first. I'll drop you at the station; I left my car there anyway." He'd left the copies of the writing-class papers at home. He'd settle down in his favorite chair and concentrate. Brenda would be out, as this was her morning at the hairdresser's. She always went on a Saturday so she'd look good for the weekend.

But she wasn't at the hairdresser's, it seemed. There was a note magneted to the refrigerator. "Dear Knute," it read, "I have gone to Hyannis for a book-buying seminar. If you recall, they've put me in charge of new purchases for the library for the coming year. I don't know why it slipped my mind—must be old age creeping up. Anyway, I should be back Sunday before noon. There's some Stouffer's entrees in the freezer or maybe you'd enjoy eating out. See you then. Brenda."

Knute grunted. This library business was getting to be a bit much. He wouldn't mind a couple of days on the Cape himself. Maybe he'd go down tomorrow if things were slow . . . but in the meantime, back to the saga of Roseanna dela Mare. Where had she left off . . . or rather, where had he left off? Brenda's note reminded him. "But the result was Victor."

Victor was a railroad man, he told Mother. He worked on crews maintaining the roadbed. He'd be gone for days at a time, riding and living in a little caboose. He wouldn't be any trouble, no trouble at all, he assured us.

He fascinated me. We had never had a man in the house. He had a swarthy complexion, black hair, a turned-up mustache and brown eyes. And polite! He said "yes, ma'am" and "no, ma'am" and stood up when my mother stood or when Aunt Jessie or Bedelia or Lily walked in. They all inspected him, then decided he would do.

Maybe, I thought, he would marry Jessie or Bedelia. Not Lily —she was too old for him. And not Dulcie, my mother—she didn't need a husband; she had too much to do already, taking care of the house and me. The first Sunday that he was there I could hardly wait to get home from Sunday school so I could see what was going on.

I told my Sunday school friend Sarah about Victor. "Is he handsome?" she wanted to know. I wasn't exactly sure but I said, "Oh, yes. Dark and handsome."

My family was on the screened-in back porch, drinking iced tea. Victor was nowhere to be seen. "Where's the roomer?" I asked.

"Gone out," said Mother.

"Maybe to church," said Grandmother.

"I doubt that." Aunt Jessie was shuffling fortune-telling cards.

"Oh, tell my fortune," I begged.

"Go change your Sunday school clothes and maybe then I will," she said.

"Oh, good!" I ran up the stairs, passing the roomer's closed door as I did so. He wasn't out, he was in; he startled me when he opened the door and said, "Good morning, Roseanna. That's your name, isn't it—Roseanna?"

"Yes, sir. Aunt Jessie is going to tell my fortune. Don't you want to come down and get your fortune told, too?"

He fingered his mustache. "I might be in the way."

Would they welcome him, I wondered? Of course they would. Someone new to talk to. He could tell us about railroads. I loved trains and one day I planned to ride on one leaving town by way of the big Union Depot and going—well, I didn't know where but somewhere far away. "You go right on down," I told him. "They're out on the back porch."

"You're all dressed up this morning." His eyes looked shiny, oily-wet. "A very pretty young lady."

I didn't know what to say. No one had ever said I was pretty before. I didn't get a chance to say anything dumb because someone was coming up the stairs. Mother.

"Something I can do for you, Mr. Hopewell?" she asked.

"Good morning, Mrs. Randolph. I was only telling Roseanna how nice she looks this morning. Been to Sunday school, I'll bet."

"Yes, and now she must run along and change her clothes. Everything all right, Mr. Hopewell? You're comfortable?" I could hear them through my closed door.

"Couldn't be better, ma'am. Nice clean sheets, plenty of towels. An old bachelor like me calls it paradise. Only thing to keep life from being hunky-dory is . . . well, I don't know how to put it . . ."

"Please go on, Mr. Hopewell."

"Well, it's home cookin'. Eatin' out in hash houses all the time, it's kind of hard on the old gut, ma'am, if you'll pardon the expression. It can give you a real bellyache."

"You mean you would like to eat with us?"

"Well, now, I don't want to be any trouble, Mrs. Randolph, I don't want to intrude but I'd be willing to pay handsomely if I could just take supper with you when I'm in town."

I had on my play dress now, so I could come out and join in the conversation. "Mother," I said, "I think that would be very neighborly. And we could use the extra income."

Victor patted me on the head. "She's not only a little beauty, she's smart, too."

"We'll see," said Mother. "Come along, Roseanna."

"We'll have to ask the others." I twisted my head to look back up the stairs at him. He smiled and nodded.

"You go too far, Roseanna," said Mother.

"But I think it would be nice. We'd have something new to

talk about at supper. And maybe he'd take a shine to Aunt Jessie or Aunt Bedelia—"

Mother stopped short and stared at me.

"Well, he might," I said lamely.

"Where do you get these ideas? At your age?"

"I've got a lot of imagination, Aunt Jessie says."

Mother sighed. We walked silently on to join the others.

The discussion about whether our roomer should become a boarder took longer than I thought. "Except for Sundays it's the only time we're all together," Bedelia pointed out. "It's our private time."

"How much did he say he'd be willing to pay?" Lily was always practical.

"He said 'handsomely'," I answered the question.

"Whatever that means." Mother put in her two cents' worth.

"What if he has dreadful table manners?" asked Aunt Jessie.

"That would be very bad for little pitchers." Bedelia shook her head doubtfully.

"I could ask him." I wanted to be helpful.

"Don't you dare!" Mother scowled.

"Could we do it on a trial basis?" asked Grandmother.

"We might." Aunt Jessie pulled her lower lip under her upper lip, as she always did when she was thinking. "Dulcie, tell him he can take supper with us on a trial basis at the cost of one dollar per supper. If either party isn't satisfied, he can eat elsewhere."

"A dollar!" Mother raised her eyebrows. "That's a lot."

"Tell him he can take it or leave it." Jessie poked her nose toward the ceiling.

Mother shook her head. "I think he'll leave it at that price."

"I hope so," said Bedelia.

"We can feed the whole family at that rate," Grandmother figured.

"He must be rich," I said.

"He's got nobody else to spend his money on." Aunt Jessie shuffled the cards. "Come on, Roseanna, let's see what the cards tell about your future this time."

I sat down beside her. "Oh, I do hope they say I'm going to marry a rich man and have six children like they did last time!"

"Shhhh," Aunt Jessie scolded me. "I'm concentrating."

And that was how Victor began to have supper with us. He'd be away for maybe ten days, at home for five, something like that. Sometimes he'd show me the brown specks on his hands. "Creosote," he'd say. "We soak the railroad ties in creosote and some of it splashes on my hands. Burns like the devil."

We learned more about him at each supper. He had no family. He'd come to our city from a sod house in western Kansas, where his father had been a wheat farmer. His father died when Victor was a boy, leaving Victor's mother with Victor and two sisters. It wasn't too long after the last of the Indian wars, and some renegade Indians came by one day, looking for anything they could steal. Victor had been out in the fields when it happened. He came home to find his mother and sisters dead and things had been done that he couldn't rightly describe to ladies. What could those things be? I wondered. I would worm it out of Aunt Jessie.

"Oh, dear." Mother had tears in her eyes. Even Bedelia, who liked Victor the least, looked sad.

"Have another piece of chicken." Grandmother passed the platter to him.

"The poor wren," murmured Jessie, "will fly against the owl when there are young ones in the nest."

"Did you write that, Aunt Jessie?" She had let me read some of her poems.

"William Shakespeare," she said. *"Macbeth*. Scene two, act four."

I could see that impressed Victor. He looked at her kind of wide-eyed. I'd decided Aunt Jessie was the one for Victor. Even though she wore eyeglasses she was a nice-looking lady. She had lots of reddish gold, wavy hair, so long that when she let it down she could sit on it. Sometimes she'd let me brush it. It made me ashamed of my own hair, which was more like Mother's and Bedelia's, very straight and blond. We were cursed with fine hair, Mother and Bedelia and me.

Then, too, Jessie had pink cheeks and light hazel eyes that could look right into you. Yes, she was a nice-looking lady and it was time she got married. I'd even heard Lily tell Mother that.

"Jessie will do things in her own sweet time," she had answered. "You know that, Mother."

Grandmother had sighed. "Indeed I do. But she's having her twenty-fifth birthday and after that—"

"Oh, yes." Mother's voice sounded funny. "After that it's all downhill to the graveyard."

"Well, after all, Dulcie, you did have a husband. And you do have Roseanna. It isn't as though no man ever . . ." Her voice trailed off.

"No, it isn't as though no man ever . . ." Mother was imitating Grandmother. "Maybe it would have been better if he hadn't."

"Don't say that, Dulcie. There's Roseanna. You wouldn't have Roseanna."

"You're right, Mother, of course. It's only that sometimes the nights are very long."

"Yes," Grandmother had agreed. "I know."

So it was clear to me that Aunt Jessie, being nearly twenty-five, was the one for Victor. But there seemed to be no spark between them. I went to Bedelia to find out why.

"Jessie? And the roomer? Good heavens, Roseanna, the things you think of. And at your tender age. What could Jessie possibly have in common with that man?"

"In common? What does that mean?"

"Liking the same things. Common interests. Like Jessie likes poetry and Shakespeare and concerts and all those things. Why, I'll bet that man never even read a book."

I thought about that. "They both like traveling. You heard them talk about traveling, going places on the railroad. Victor's been all the way to Galveston. And Chicago. You can't say they don't have that in common."

"Jessie hasn't been anywhere. But if she did she'd have more to say about Galveston than that all the streets are straight and more about Chicago than it's got lots of bridges. What you have in mind is matching up a peacock with a crow."

Aunt Jessie? A peacock? I'd never seen a peacock but I'd seen lots of crows and it was true—in the bird world Victor could have been a crow with his sleek black hair.

"Here." Aunt Bedelia handed me a package. "Your *Tip Top Weekly* came. I've got to leave for work. Tell your mother I may be late for supper. It's the end of the month."

Tip Top Weekly, "An Ideal Publication for American Youth," featured my hero, Frank Merriwell. Frank Merriwell was the kind of man I would marry . . . "his handsome proportions, his graceful, muscular figure, his fine, kingly head and that look of clean manliness stamped him as a fellow of lofty thoughts and ambitions . . ."

I had my *Tip Top Weekly* under my arm as I climbed the stairs to my room. Victor's door opened. "Oh, Roseanna," he said, "I thought you were your mother. I was just going to ask her for another quilt. I'm feeling chilly and the nights are getting colder."

"Mother's out at the grocery store and everyone else has gone to work. I know where she keeps the quilts. I'll get you one."

"Would you, please? That's a good girl." He shivered and hugged himself. "Maybe I'm coming down with something."

"I'll be right back," I promised. I put my *Tip Top Weekly* in my room and went up to the attic. The quilts were kept in a big wooden storage box. Some of them had been made by Great-grandmother Evelyn. Where was she now? I wondered. Could she see me? Did she know I was thinking about her? In Sunday school Miss Denbow said that whenever you remembered someone who had left this vale of tears you were keeping them alive. Every night when I said my prayers I named everybody I could think of: all my family, my father, my friends, even Abraham Lincoln. I got the quilt and went downstairs.

Victor's door was shut. I knocked on it.

"Come in," he said.

I went in with the quilt.

Victor was lying in bed, all covered up.

"Maybe you *are* coming down with something," I said. "Want me to cover you up with this?"

"Yes. Please."

I went up to the bed and unfolded the quilt. Suddenly he threw the covers off him. He was stark naked.

He said, "I hurt there." He pointed. "Would you rub it for me? You would be doing such a good deed." His voice sounded funny, thick like syrup.

I turned to go to the door but he reached out and grabbed my arm.

"Rub," he said, holding my arm tighter, forcing me to lean

over him. He put his other hand on my hip, pulling me onto the bed.

"Don't," I said.

"Rub!" He was pulling me, pulling me down. I tried to get loose but I couldn't.

He was forcing me down, lower, lower, it was getting closer and closer, bigger and bigger right before my eyes.

I threw up. All over him.

Then I ran to the bathroom, where there was a key in the lock. I locked the door. I kept it locked no matter how hard he pounded, no matter what he said.

As soon as Mother came home, I told her. Victor was gone that night and we never had another roomer.

Aunt Jessie met James Jenruth at the Boston Store's company outing. Every Fourth of July the Boston Store had a big company picnic in Riverside Park that lasted all day. When it got dark they showed moving pictures on a big screen so everybody could see. After that, fireworks! Aunt Jessie said that when I got old enough I could go, too. All the families were invited but Lily and Mother didn't care to go, and to tell the truth I suspected that Jessie and Bedelia didn't want to bother with me. Aunt Jessie always brought me something, though—a small American flag, a red, white and blue badge, a paper hat with a ribbon.

It was the year she brought me the hat that she also brought us James Jenruth. Not that very night, of course, but he came the next Sunday, wearing a blue-and-white-striped shirt with red-and-blue suspenders and a blue tie. On his head he wore a straw sailor hat with a red ribbon. I guessed that was the outfit he'd worn for the Fourth of July and he wasn't ready to give it up.

Jessie acted as though she hadn't expected him at all, but I noticed she was wearing her new white voile shirt-waist with all the embroidery on the bodice and hem of the skirt (seven whole dollars ready-made at the Boston Store!) and that she'd left off her glasses.

After Jessie had introduced him, Grandmother announced that she had mending to do; could she be excused? Aunt Bedelia was going to a friend's house to look at a new dress pattern. I wondered what friend she meant but didn't bother to ask. I was too interested in the man Aunt Jessie had brought home. His eyes were blue, but sort of a faded blue; either that or the bright blue of his tie made them look that way.

Mother broke into my study (he had curly hair, sort of straw-colored, and freckles) with, "Roseanna and I are going to the ice cream parlor. Can we bring some back for you?"

The ice cream parlor? Golly. Well, maybe we could hurry. I wondered what Jessie and James Jenruth would talk about, what they had in common. How could I learn anything in an ice cream parlor? Still, an ice cream soda . . . I went with Mother without an argument.

"She didn't even mention him." Mother may have been talking to herself. "Who do you suppose he could be?"

"Maybe an employee of the Boston Store." I took a couple of skips. "Do you think he's handsome?"

"Not handsome. I wouldn't call him handsome. But manly, maybe. Yes, I'd say manly."

Manly. Like Frank Merriwell. I ate my soda as fast as I could but by the time we got back he had gone. Aunt Jessie kind of bristled when I asked about him.

"He's a cousin of Mrs. Bidderman." The Biddermans owned the Boston Store. "A cousin from Eureka. His father was her mother's half brother."

"That makes him a half cousin," I said.

Jessie glared at me. "I don't know why you all are so excited. He was in the neighborhood and merely stopped by."

"Is he going to stay in this city?" Grandmother wanted to know. I wasn't the only one who was curious.

"He's accepted a job at the Boston Store. In shipping. He says he wants to learn the business from the bottom up."

"Gee, Aunt Jessie, is he rich like the Biddermans?"

"That's enough of that, Roseanna." When Mother sounded like that I knew enough to shut up.

Jessie stood up, gathered her white, embroidered skirt around her like a queen and started to leave. At the door she looked back. "I don't know why but he seems to like me. I find him pleasant. That's all there is to it for now. Don't push me, please. I'll tell you if there's ever anything to tell."

At Christmas she told us. "James has proposed marriage. I'm considering his proposal."

Nobody said anything. We didn't want to push her, we'd agreed, in any direction.

"He isn't good enough for her" was Bedelia's privately expressed opinion.

"I just hope he's well off," Lily hoped aloud. "He could be a poor relation, you know. And all this 'learning the business from the ground up' could be so much malarkey. It could be that's all he is and ever will be, a shipping clerk."

"She's different when he's around," my mother mused. "Softer, do you know what I mean? Not so—anxious."

"Anxious? What's Aunt Jessie got to be anxious about?" That didn't make sense to me but nobody explained and now here was Aunt Jessie telling us that she was thinking about getting married.

"Well." Jessie looked at each of us. "Don't you have anything to say?"

"You didn't say you were going to marry him. You just said you were considering it," I pointed out.

"There are perceptive people who would take that to mean that advice might be accepted." Jessie's cheeks were pinker than usual.

"I don't see how we can advise you," Grandmother spoke

stiffly. "He's been a forbidden topic of discussion. We don't really know very much about him."

"If I'm in love with him, I'd think that would be all you'd need to know." Her voice was rising with each sentence.

"Are you in love with him?" asked Mother.

Aunt Jessie looked down at her lap. "I don't know."

"Then that should be the answer," Bedelia snapped. "If you don't know, then you aren't."

Aunt Jessie looked straight at her. "I think I am."

"Well, then," I said, "I agree with Aunt Jessie. If she loves him, that should be enough for us. I trust her judgment. Don't you?"

"Jessie," Mother spoke softly. "What's holding you back?"

"Nothing, really. I—He's younger than I am. By two years. Sometimes it seems even more than that. He thinks like a little boy sometimes."

"I read where all men are little boys at heart." I was trying to be helpful.

Grandmother reached out and patted Jessie's shoulder. "It's hard for women with strong personalities to find husbands who are stronger. I think that's because that type of man is attracted to the weaker type of woman. Perhaps we are attracted, likewise, to the weaker type of man. Perhaps it runs in the family."

I certainly hoped not. I wanted a man like Frank Merriwell. "Was Grandfather Staley a weak man, Grandmother?"

"He had his problems." Her hand was still on Jessie's shoulder.

"What about my father?"

"He wasn't old enough to reap a good crop."

"What are James' problems, Aunt Jessie?"

She looked at me. "I don't know yet."

"Isn't that kind of scary?"

She frowned.

"I mean, if you knew what they were you could say, 'Well, I can put up with that.' But if you don't know what they are, maybe they'll be things you can't put up with. Are you sure there will be problems?"

She nodded. "Pretty sure."

I didn't think that was the way to do things. I thought the best thing was to pick out a perfect man as soon as you could and, by planning every step of the way, end up living happily ever after. If you were smart and put your mind to it you could surely get it right the first time. All it took was making your mind up.

"I think I shall accept him," Aunt Jessie was saying. "He makes me feel—like smiling when I'm with him. I can't ask for more than that, can I? So I think I'll accept him."

"May I be the flower girl?" I could hardly wait for my first wedding.

James moved in with us after the wedding, "just for the time being. Until we get enough saved to buy our own house. I want a real swell house for Jessie. She deserves the best and if we live here for a while we can get it much quicker. God knows I wish I had a fortune to drop at her feet 'stead of being just a poor relation of the Biddermans."

But the little while turned into a longer while and a war began across the ocean because somebody shot somebody royal in a place called Sarajevo, Yugoslavia. We didn't pay much attention to that; we had more important things to think about. Aunt Jessie and Uncle James bought a Model T Ford and Aunt Bedelia joined the Political Equality Association, whose slogan was "Votes for Women."

And Eubanke Dewing showed up.

He came to our door on a summer morning carrying two large cases, a big camera and a pipelike arrangement he called a tripod. Mother answered the door. I could see her from the kitchen, where I was shelling black-eyed peas. He removed his derby hat and handed her his card. It read (I discovered later): EUBANKE DEWING, Professional Photographer specializing in family portraits in your own home.

"Oh, dear." Mother was wearing an apron over her housedress and a kerchief over her hair. She'd been on her way to the backyard to beat the parlor carpet. "I'm afraid we aren't all here for a family portrait even if we wanted one."

"I quite understand." He sounded like an actor rather than an ordinary man. "Perhaps we could make an appointment for some time when your husband is at home."

"Oh, no. I mean, well, I'm a widow. It's my mother and sisters. And my brother-in-law. I mean, if we were to have a family portrait they'd have to be here and they aren't."

I came down the hall a little way to see and hear better. "And this must be another of your sisters," said Eubanke Dewing, peering around the screen door at me.

"Oh, no. That's my daughter." The back of Mother's neck was pink and I knew she was blushing. I took a sudden dislike to Mr. Eubanke Dewing. Him and his la-de-dah way.

"We've got pictures," I said. "We've got our own Kodak. We take pictures all the time."

Actually we'd used the camera twice in the past few months, once to photograph the new automobile and the second time to capture Aunt Bedelia in her suffragist outfit. She had a red, white and blue sash running across her chest with VOTES FOR WOMEN printed on it in gilt letters, and she carried a handmade sign that said HELP US WIN THE VOTE. She had on her best hat, like a bowl of flowers with a brim, and wore her best suit and her new high-button shoes.

"Maybe you could come around this evening and speak to my sister and her husband," Mother was saying to Eubanke Dewing, photographer, just as though I hadn't spoken.

"I don't think they'll be coming home after work tonight," I blurted. "I think Aunt Jessie said they might be going to Chautauqua tonight. Harry Fogelman is going to be speaking. He speaks a hundred words a minute, so they say."

"Roseanna"—Mother hardly ever used that tone—"have you finished what you were doing in the kitchen? No? Well, then go finish it." And so I had to leave, as I told Aunt Bedelia later, I had to allow her to make an appointment with that—that— "lounge lizard?" Bedelia suggested.

"Yes. Lounge lizard. I'll bet he is. He had on one of those jackets with pleats and a belt in the back. And leather puttees around his pant legs."

"Goodness." Bedelia looked impressed. Bedelia had been very taken with motion pictures so she added, "Like Cecil B. De Mille." She'd begun to put her hair up in rags every night for the purpose of having long ringlets like Mary Pickford and I had tried it, too, but after an hour or so my ringlets became limp hanks of hair so I stuck to my braids.

But I must have put it up for the family portrait that Eubanke Dewing took because there I sit, between Mother and Grandmother on the front steps of our house, with Aunt Jessie and Uncle James and Aunt Bedelia sitting on the higher steps behind, and I've got wavy hair. I'm smiling, kind of a leering smile; Mother has the most serene look on her face; Grandmother looks regal; and the others look deadly serious. It was years later before I realized what a good photograph Eubanke Dewing had taken. At that time, all I could think about was how much I hated him.

"He's after my mother," I told my school friend Bertha, "and she likes him, I can tell. I don't know why, but she does. She's invited him to Sunday dinner!"

"Maybe he'll go away soon. Before it's too late." Bertha didn't like him because I didn't like him. That's how friends are. She gave me hope.

But he didn't go and Mother became Dulcie Dewing in a pretty pongee gown and picture hat to match. I'd refused to go to the wedding but Grandmother said I'd break my mother's heart and Aunt Jessie pointed out that if I disliked Eubanke Dewing so much I'd be giving him cause to come between my mother and me. Bedelia snorted and said she was inclined to agree with me but if Mother wanted to be a fool and get married again that was her business, to which James replied that he didn't think it was so foolish to get married and as far as he was concerned Eubanke wasn't such a bad fella. The result was that I went to the wedding but I kept my eyes on the floor so I wouldn't see him kiss her at the end.

That was the end of Roseanna's tale. Knute put the pages together and fastened them with a paper clip. He'd learned that the victim had been a precocious young woman with resentment toward her new stepfather. Alice Buono was supposed to look up newspaper stories concerning Roseanna Randolph dela Mare. She'd have a report when he went back to the office this afternoon and maybe that would throw some light on the subject.

Evangeline Meeny had entitled her pages "The Story of My Life." Knute picked up where he'd left off.

The first obstacle in my life was me. I didn't look like other people and I didn't think like other people. That was a problem. I got very good grades in school because I had nothing else to do but study. I didn't have boyfriends and I didn't have girl-friends either. My mother had died when I was a baby so all I had was a father. He was elderly. I had been born when he was forty-two.

Besides studying, I had a lot of time to think. I had time to think about my obstacle, and what to do about it. It took me quite a while to figure it out—years, in fact. It wasn't until I was in high school that I decided to marry Francis Xaviar Meeny.

Some might have considered my ambition an impossible one. Francis was the president of our class; he was tall, handsome and charming; and he'd been going steady with Phyllis Gore for two years. Phyllis was the president of the honor society and, according to our yearbook, "Miss Best Dressed" as well as "Miss Best Dancer." Naturally, Francis was "Mr. Best Dancer." I was "Evangeline Dwyer, nicknamed Vangie, member of the Honor Society, the Stamp Club, the Latin Club, the Future Homemak-ers' Club. Vangie will listen to a friend's problems anytime."

The last statement became the solution to my obstacle and my road to success. I practiced on other people but I was really working up to listening to Francis Xaviar Meeny, who lived two houses from me, and who was worried about a great many things the summer right after graduation.

Such as finding a job. And whether or not Phyllis Gore was pregnant. And what would happen when Phyllis Gore (not pregnant) went off to teachers' college in the fall. And how to make do on twelve dollars a week when you gave your mother half of that for room and board. We spent many an evening sitting in the swing on my front porch solving Francis' problems one way or another.

It took time. The first Christmas vacation, when Phyllis came home from teachers' college, nearly tore my fancy web to pieces but they had a fight between Christmas and New Year's. I commiserated while she went out with a fellow college student home for the holidays, and that was more or less the end of that.

Of course, it wasn't as simple as I make it sound. Francis went out and got drunk and I was fortunate enough to be the one he came to to sober up before his mother caught him and that helped the cause. You wonder what my father was doing while all this was going on? Well, as I said, he was getting along in years and neither his hearing nor his eyesight was very good and frankly I don't think he cared.

The result of all this was, dear reader, as Jane Eyre said so eloquently, I married him. Evangeline Dwyer became Evangeline Meeny in front of a priest and two witnesses and Francis' mother and my father and maybe a half dozen of Francis' coworkers. He didn't want a big wedding, he said. He didn't want to invite the whole world. Did I mind? No, I didn't mind. I had him; that's what mattered. Ten months later, Roger was born on his father's birthday. The world was mine.

Six months later my darling, my beautiful husband, was dead.

> Obili si ergo
> Fortibusesin ero
> Nobilis demis trux
> Si watzin em
> Cowsand dux.

Translated from the Latin: O, Bili see 'er go, forti buses in a ro, No, Bili dem is trux, see what's in 'em, cows an' dux.

I knew everybody in the movies—not only the stars but also the entire cast, their names, who they were married to, or had been married to. The only thing I didn't know was that so many of my favorites were Jewish. Like Danny Kaye.

Do you think Bob Hope will still be telling those jokes into the twenty-first century?

Knute clipped Evangeline Meeny together. One more to go. Ward Butler. What did he have to say on those neatly typed pages?

My first conquest was in high school. I played on both the football team and the baseball team and there was something about being an athlete that made it surprisingly easy. I didn't know whether to be pleased or disappointed. The girl I had thought was such a nice girl wasn't. When I found out, I wondered if they were all that way. I found out they pretty much were.

I've been married three times. The first time I was very young. She really fooled me. She'd held out and I thought, boy oh boy, I'd found a fine one. She was pure, all right—I wasn't wrong about that—but she had other faults. Looking back, I feel I was damned lucky to escape from that one.

The second one was a real beauty. All my life I've been a sucker for beauty. Beauty of face and form or beauty of sky and land; beauty is found in symmetry. The trouble is that much of the beauty in this world has vanished. The way people dress now and the things they do to their hair and their figures and their minds . . . Anyway, the second one was so lovely to look at I couldn't resist. Golden curls, eyes like opals, cherry lips, the figure of a goddess. And the greediest, most grasping mind you ever came across. All she wanted was more, more, more. I had the devil's own time getting out of that one. Turned out that I refused to pay her alimony and went to jail rather than do that! Six months I served. Jail! That's another story.

My third wife is the one I'm married to now. Amanda has been Mrs. Butler for over thirty years. She's not much to look at and nothing special to talk to but she's easy to live with and she keeps a good house.

Above all else I wish there were more beauty in the world. And manners. Walking on the outside when you escort a lady down the street. Standing up to be introduced. Tipping your hat. Nobody even wears hats anymore unless their ears are freezing.

I wish there were more beauty in the world. Does that sound foolish? Well, it isn't!

There are levels of pain so there must be levels of fear.

I wonder if the two go hand in hand?

I have a high threshold of pain and a high threshold of fear. But that may be because I've never been physically hurt nor truly frightened. Not even when behind those rigid bars.

The most horrifying tales I've heard are these:

Question—how do you skin a pig (man?) alive without him squealing his head off?

Answer—first cut out his tongue.

Long, long ago (maybe not that long) in Egypt or India or one of those places where baby girls were considered a curse rather than a blessing, they used to sew up their orifices and that is how they slowly died.

There was a happy time and everyone was laughing and singing and dancing on the grass when an unseen evil moved among them and poisoned their grass and one by one they fell like dominoes . . .

We had a cat named Charlie. We had other cats in our time

but this is about Charlie. Pardon, *we* didn't have Charlie—it was more like *he* had *us.*

Charlie was totally white, with golden eyes. His physique was elegant: fine-boned, heavily muscled but a pleasure to look upon, a delight in motion. And intelligent. We talked to him and he talked back but he didn't ask stupid questions.

He washed a lot. It was difficult to be a white cat, he said. But he managed—until a car hit him. Dead, he was—soiled.

He was killed by a careless driver because *he* was careless. He was chasing another cat who'd been annoying him.

We miss Charlie.

If we could, we would poison the other cat.

Or shoot the driver of the car that killed Charlie.

We buried Charlie in the sand by the sea.

He was so beautiful, white with golden eyes, and—for a cat—he laughed a lot.

Knute shook his head and paper-clipped Edward Butler. So much for the inner thoughts of possible murder suspects. So far as he could figure it out, reading all that stuff had been a total waste of time. He couldn't see any reason for looking for needles in similar haystacks.

The voice on the other end of the telephone line said, "Hello? Mr. Severson? Knute Severson there?"

"I'm here." What the hell time was it? Middle of the night. It was black outside, not morning gray.

"I'm Sergeant Kessler, State Police. I'm sorry to get you up but—there's been an accident."

Knute sat erect. "Leif? My son Leif?"

"No, not your son. It's your wife, Brenda Severson, that's your wife, isn't it? There was an ID card in her purse."

"Brenda? In an accident? Is she—she isn't—dead?"

"Not yet. I mean, no, but it's critical. She's at Jordan Hospital in Plymouth. Apparently she was on her way back from the Cape . . . the car she was riding in crossed the median. It's our guess that the driver was under the influence or just went to sleep. We'll know after the autopsy."

"The driver is dead? Who was the driver?"

"Name's Randolph Harper." Knute recognized the deliberate noncommittal tone; he'd used it himself on occasion.

"Randolph Harper?" For a minute he had to think who he was . . . yes, the library trustee who'd called . . . "She's at Jordan Hospital, you said? I'm coming right down. An hour, maybe less. I'm on my way."

"Be careful—you don't want to crack up, too."

"I'll use the siren. This time I'll use the siren."

"The siren?"

"Yes. I'm Chief Severson. Chief of Police Severson. I'll be there as soon as humanly possible."

He looked at her as he would look at a stranger. Caucasian female. Hair, black. Well, so dark a brown that it looked black. Eyes. He couldn't see the eyes beneath the closed lids but he knew. Brown. Sometimes a warm, laughing brown; sometimes a shooting-sparks brown. Age, forty-two. Too young to be lying there. Given name Brenda, maiden name Purdue, married name Severson. Occupation, wife, mother . . . He'd have to call Leif. No, better to go there, tell him face-to-face, bring him back to his mother's funeral. She had died between the time of the phone call and his arrival. Even though he had used the siren.

He made a sound, a sound he didn't know he could make. (Don't do that, someone will hear.) He didn't want anyone to hear and yet he couldn't stop the sound, the noise, the—bawling. That's what the sound was, loud and deep and ugly.

He groped for a handkerchief in his hip pocket and stuffed it in his mouth like a gag. A part of his mind told him this is what it feels like losing someone, this is what it feels like when someone you love dies.

He hadn't known.

It rained for the funeral.

His mother and father flew up from Florida. They wanted to take Leif back with them until school started again but Leif said no, much as he'd like to, he'd committed himself as a counselor at the summer camp and if he didn't go back they'd be short a counselor. He couldn't go back on his word.

He's growing up, thought Knute. His mother would have been proud of him for thinking that way.

Knute had had a phone call from Lawrence Benedict, his partner when they were both on the Boston police force long ago—when they were young. Benedict called from the Caribbean island of St. Martin, where he had lived the past few years, and said that he'd heard the dreadful news through a tourist from Wellesley. "It's a funny thing about this island," Benedict had said, "you hear things here so fast—news comes on the wind. God, Knute, we're sorry. What can we do? Anything?"

"I— Thanks for calling, Benedict. How's the family?"

"Fine. Fine. Barbara gets to swim every day; it's done her a world of good. Kim is at Duke, doing very well, too. Is Leif all right, your mother and father okay?"

"All right. Yes, all right. We're all all right. Today we're all right. Tomorrow— Yes, we'll be all right. God, Benedict, I sound like a babbling idiot."

"How did it happen?"

Knute told him.

"Damn. That's a horrible thing, really terrible. You know how Barbara and I feel . . ."

"Yes, thanks." He was running out of words.

"Hey, can you take some time off? Come down and visit us? It's quiet here this time of year and—"

"I don't know, Lawrence, I just don't know."

"Of course you don't. Think about it. All you have to do is let me know and we'll meet you at the airport. That's all. In the meantime, hang in there, friend, hang in there."

"I will."

He would—at least he would *try.*

There were papers on his desk, piled in the IN basket waiting to be passed to the OUT basket but he couldn't find the energy to tackle them. Somebody should take them out and run them through the computer. The computer would have all the answers, God knows he didn't . . . Breathe deep, lean back, take your time, you'll get back on track, it just takes time, time . . . His telephone rang.

"Chief Severson," he said into it.

"Sir, there's a lady here to see you." Officer Buono's tone was close to a whisper.

"I'm not . . ." He didn't know what he was about to say. I'm not available? I'm not ready? I'm not seeing anybody?

"It's Mrs. Harper," Officer Buono murmured.

"Mrs. Randolph Harper?"

"Yes, sir."

He breathed deeply and leaned back in his chair. "Send her in." He closed his eyes. This was going to be awful. But he had to see her. He had to see the missing part of the puzzle, the other piece of the why . . .

The door opened and a slim, pale woman came in. Her hair

was silver blond and her eyes a brilliant blue. They were the only brilliant thing about her. Everything else was pale and muted: the beige of her clothing, the whiteness of her skin, the faded pink of her mouth, the tonelessness of her voice.

"I had to come. I'm sorry, but I had to come."

Knute stood up and made a gesture with his hand. He didn't know what he meant by it. "Please sit down, Mrs. Harper."

Why? he wondered. Why? You're a pretty lady. You look like a nice lady. Why did your husband take my wife? Why, Mrs. Harper?

"Why," asked Mrs. Harper, "did your wife want my husband? Do you know why?"

"Do you have children?"

She blinked; the hypnotist had snapped his fingers. "Twin girls. They're twelve. Almost thirteen."

"My son is sixteen. He's—devastated."

"The girls, too. Devastated."

They were still standing. He said again, "Please sit down." She sat and so did he. What to say?

"I had to see you." Her eyes were so wide they seemed stretched. "I had to see if you were the reason. Only how can you tell?"

"I don't know." Are you? Do you know? "How can you tell?" Was he staring at her as she was staring at him?

Suddenly she was on her feet again. "I'm sorry. I'm very sorry."

"I'm sorry, too." He wasn't sure if she heard—the door shut before he got it out. He fell back in his chair, feeling drained and melancholy and a little sick.

Officer Buono had attached a note to the computer printout she'd left on his desk. The note read: "Roseanna dela Mare was born Roseanna Randolph in Kansas. I called the sheriff's office in her hometown and asked for background. Here's what they sent. The first article on the picnic was on the front page of the local paper on July 6, 1927; the follow-up on July 10, same year. The dela Mare article is from the Boston *Globe,* started on the first page and continued on the obituary page on August 28, 1973; the second article is dated three days later; the third two days following that."

The 1927 headline announced: POISONED FOOD KILLS PIC-NICKERS, with the subhead "Entire Family Wiped Out at 4th of July Celebration."

Eleven picnickers died agonizing deaths on Wednesday after eating contaminated food at a Fourth of July celebration sponsored by the Boston Store the well-known local emporium.

Almost the entire family of longtime employee Jessie Staley Jenruth expired along with five friends who had partaken of the same picnic fare. It was Boston Store policy for employees to bring special culinary dishes to augment the store-provided menu of barbecued chicken and ribs. The Jenruth group brought two large containers, one of potato salad and one of cole slaw, and two thermos bottles, one of tea, one of lemonade. Doctors at Wesleyan Hospital were of the opinion that the potato salad became contaminated in the ninety-degree heat. Tests are under way.

Jessie Staley Jenruth had been employed by the Boston Store for twenty-two years, as a bookkeeper. Her husband, James Jenruth, was in charge of the shipping department and was a cousin of Mrs. Ernestine Bidderman, wife of Boston Store owner Albert Bidderman.

Also deceased were Mrs. Jenruth's mother, Mrs. Lily Staley, for many years an employee of the Kellihay Packing Company; Mrs. Jenruth's sisters, Mrs. Dulcie Randolph Dewing and Miss Bedelia Staley; and Mrs. Dewing's husband, the photographer Eubanke Dewing.

Also among the deceased but not members of the Jenruth-Staley family were coworkers George Pincher, Mary Elizabeth Carson, Bertha Sue Boudine, Ralph M. Hinkle and Louisa May Alexander.

Funeral arrangements for the victims will be made when the autopsies are completed.

Another member of the Jenruth-Staley family escaped a similar fate. Roseanna Randolph (daughter of Dulcie Randolph Dewing and the late Mr. Randolph) was on her honeymoon with Frederick B. Kirby, the well-known baseball player. They are expected to return immediately.

The follow-up article was headlined PICNIC FOOD LACED WITH SILVER NITRATE: Dead Picnickers Met with Foul Play.

Dr. Richard Albritton of the county coroner's office announced today that he had found traces of silver nitrate in the bodies of the Jenruth-Staley family and five friends who died July 4 following the ingestion of homemade potato salad at the Boston Store annual picnic. Dr. Albritton added that the potato salad, when analyzed, revealed the presence of a heavy dose of silver bromide, a nitrate-based chemical used in the practice of photography. Mr. Eubanke Dewing, one of the victims, was a professional photographer and had a studio in the family home.

According to Dr. Albritton, silver bromide is used in negative emulsions. They consist of suspensions in gelatin containing silver nitrate, which is then run into a solution of potassium bromide, thus creating silver bromide.

Silver nitrate is a poison causing violent abdominal pains, vomiting and diarrhea. These were the symptoms evidenced by the deceased, according to witnesses.

Mrs. Roseanna Kirby, the only surviving member of the Jenruth-Staley-Dewing family, is reported to be under a doctor's care. She returned yesterday from Galveston, where she had been on her honeymoon. Her husband of a few days, Frederick B. Kirby, told this newspaper that his bride was "beside herself. All she does is cry." Mr. Kirby is a former high school third baseman recently signed following graduation to a professional baseball contract by the Boston Red Sox. He said that he had to report to the team within the week and that he hoped his wife would be able to accompany him. "If she can't, I'll just have to go alone," Mr. Kirby said sadly. "She'll have to follow as soon as she is able."

Chief of Detectives Jack Connors said there were no clues to the identity or the motive of the poisoner. "There is a quantity of silver bromide in the late Eubanke Dewing's darkroom studio but we don't know if any is missing. It doesn't look like it could have been an accident. There's no trace of the stuff in the kitchen, and the darkroom is in the cellar of the house."

Funeral services for Mr. and Mrs. James Jenruth, Mrs. Lily Staley, Mr. and Mrs. Eubanke Dewing and Miss Bedelia Staley are planned for Saturday at 2 P.M. at the Methodist Episcopal

Church. Announcement of services for George Pincher, Mary Elizabeth Carson, Bertha Sue Boudine, Ralph M. Hinkle and Louisa May Alexander can be found on the obituary page of this newspaper.

Knute jotted down the names Pincher, Carson, Boudine, Hinkle and Alexander, scrawling a big question mark beside them. Then he picked up the 1973 newspaper article.

SEAFOOD TYCOON MISSING, he read.

Coast Guard spokesmen confirmed a report that Arnold dela Mare, millionaire frozen food processor, is missing at sea. His twenty-eight-foot boat, *Sea Rose,* was found drifting yesterday evening in Cape Cod Bay.

His wife, Roseanna dela Mare, told this reporter that her husband had gone sailing in the afternoon, alone. "He often sailed by himself," she said. "The *Sea Rose* has all the latest gadgets and he's a capable sailor. He likes to sail alone," she added, "because it gives him time to think. That's what he always said. And he likes to be on the ocean. Back to his roots, he calls it. I'm quite sure he will be found. He's an excellent swimmer."

Mr. dela Mare is chief executive officer of Fine Catch, Inc., purveyors and packagers of frozen seafoods sold in supermarkets throughout the U.S.

Following that, Knute read: DELA MARE DROWNS: SUICIDE?

The body of entrepreneur Arnold dela Mare washed up on a rocky shore of Cape Cod Bay yesterday and police are asking whether his drowning was an accident or suicide. An autopsy is being performed by Medical Examiner Harold Cackus.

Mr. dela Mare disappeared from his ketch *Sea Rose* on August 29. The boat drifted ashore in the early evening. His wife, the well-known society hostess Roseanna dela Mare, expressed confidence at the time in her husband's swimming ability and said she was sure he would be found alive. Sergeant Tom Dorsey said that dela Mare was noted for his nautical prowess. He was raised in Onset and it was because of his seagoing skill that the force was entertaining ideas of possible suicide. Nothing was found amiss on the *Sea Rose*, he added. Everything on the twenty-eight-foot ketch was "shipshape." Weather conditions were good.

According to her doctor, local physician B. L. Mills, Mrs. dela Mare is in seclusion. The dela Mares were married for thirty years and have a son, Gordon, and a granddaughter, Victoria.

The last item, in smaller type, read: DELA MARE DROWNING TERMED ACCIDENT.

Authorities have ruled the death of Arnold dela Mare, millionaire frozen food processor, an accident after the results of an autopsy revealed that dela Mare had suffered a concussion prior to his death by drowning.

Police Sergeant Tom Dorsey announced the finding of the autopsy and told reporters that dela Mare, who was alone on his boat, must have slipped and fallen, striking his head in the process, then toppled into the sea.

Funeral arrangements are pending.

So, thought Knute, the late Roseanna dela Mare had lost her family and then her husband in tragic accidents. Wait a minute —someone had said something about Arnold dela Mare and sleeping pills. Nothing here about pills. And what, he wondered, had happened to third baseman Kirby? What was his first name, Fred? He made another note to check Fenway Park PR for the whereabouts of Fred Kirby. Had he met with an accident, too? A lot of coincidental tragic accidents.

It could have been an accident that silver bromide ended up in the potato salad. And it was ruled an accident that the dela Mare man had fallen into the sea. So what did that have to do with the price of tea in China? Or the frozen body of an old woman years later? So what did it have to do with anything?

So who cares? In the whole bloody scheme of things, who cares?

He pushed his chair back, stood, then walked to the window. It was raining again. What was this—Noah time? And here he was without an ark.

For the first time in his life he didn't care.

About anything.

Alice Buono, washing her hair in the shower, was regretting the fact that she'd agreed to go out with Brad Preston. True, he was really good-looking and he had a fabulous car (as well as a great line) but he also made her uncomfortable.

For one thing, the way they'd met. She'd been on Route 9 patrol with Officer Harrison Hersholt ("Harry to my friends, who are legion. American Legion") when they'd spotted this red Jaguar going like a bat (that was Harry's phrase) so they pulled it over and ticketed the driver, who turned out to be Bradford G. Preston, resident of Beacon Hill, Boston. Alice had done the ticket writing and while she was doing that he'd said things like "Sorry, ma'am, I've been out of the country and I can't get used to this fifty-five-mile limit," and "I assure you it won't happen again. I've never had one of these before; how do I handle it?" And "I can't quite read your name. Officer—Buono, is it?"

And he had telephoned. Two nights later. "I traced you down, did a little detective work on my own. I hope you don't mind. I'd like very much to take you to dinner. Any objections?"

She couldn't think of any at the time so she'd said yes. But now that it was about to happen, she was—not nervous really, only uncomfortable. But only a little. To tell the truth, she was quite flattered.

When the time came, he came to the door looking fine and was polite to her mother without being patronizing. He helped her into the Jag the old-fashioned way and took her to Ken's

Steak House, where he said he wanted to know everything about her.

"You're Alice Buono and you live with your mother on Oakencroft Road and you're twenty-four or twenty-five years old. That's all I know; now take it from there."

So she took it from there. "I've got four brothers, all older, all in the construction business, all married; I've got twelve nieces and nephews. My mother's retired. She was a housekeeper for the Abbotts. We lived on their estate so I grew up on a hundred acres by the river. My father was greenhouse man for them. When they retired they got divorced. Don't ask me why. I graduated from Wellesley High and studied at Northeastern, and now I'm a cop. That's all there is to tell." And now, she thought, tell me who *you* are.

"I'm a newsman," he said while slicing his steak. "I'm just back from Europe. I'm kind of out of touch with things back here." He grinned at her. "You can bring me up to date."

"A newsman?"

"Free-lance. Specializing in Northern Ireland. I've been living in Belfast for a year and a half. Believe me, that will put you out of touch with *everything.* Now, where shall we go, what shall we do? What's new in the theatre, movies, art, politics? What's the style in state-of-the-art U.S.A. violence? Who's mugging whom and for what? What's the biggest news in the Wellesley crime scene? What's disturbing suburbia? And all that kind of jazz."

"Is that why you asked me out? Because I'm a cop?"

He raised dark eyebrows. "Heaven forbid. I asked you out because you looked cuddly. Are you?"

She considered the question. "I don't know. I haven't found out yet."

The eyebrows moved even higher.

"My, my," he said. "We really must get acquainted."

He is, she thought while munching on salad, the most exciting man I've ever met. That should scare me. It does but it excites me more. No matter what happens it beats going bowling with Ricky Cappabianco. She drained her wineglass and nodded when Brad offered her a refill. Turn on the siren, she thought, and put the pedal to the metal, it's going to be a bumpy ride.

The coffeepot was empty when Alice got to the station the next morning. Why was it always empty when she needed a cup of hot, black coffee the most? Not that she was hung over exactly. She was tired from lack of sleep but she didn't feel too bad really. Just in need of a battery recharge. Like a cup of coffee and a kind word and maybe . . .

Her telephone rang.

"I'd like to report a theft. Someone stole my heart away. How are you, Alice of Wonderland? This is, of course, the Knave of Hearts. What time shall I pick you up this evening?"

She could see him. Hair? Bronze-colored. Skin? Tanned. Eyes? Hazel, no, almost golden. And catlike. Like a tiger's. A sleek jungle animal much too dangerous to hunt without a license.

"Seven o'clock? I should be ready by seven," said her foolhardy mouth.

"With bells on." He chuckled and hung up. She hung up more slowly. Out of her depth. No question about it. Wonderful!

But what would she wear?

"Officer Buono, could you come into my office, please?" Chief Severson was standing in his open doorway. He looked terrible, with dark circles beneath his eyes. Poor man. What a horrible thing to lose one's wife in an accident like that. She wished she could think of a way to make him feel better.

"Good morning, sir. I was just about to make some fresh coffee. Would you like a cup?" She smiled her daughterly smile.

"Yes. Okay. Thanks." And he shut his door before anyone else could get his attention. He'd been avoiding everyone these past few days, moving like a zombie, speaking only when spoken to. If he'd called her into his office, that must be a good sign. She hurried with the coffee.

"I've located this Fred Kirby," the chief told her after an experimental sip. "He lives out in Holliston, on a farm. Chief Riggins says he lives all alone which is why I've been unable to reach him on the telephone. He must be out in the fields, off somewhere. I thought I'd drive out and see if I can round him up. I'd like you to come with me."

"Kirby? The baseball player Roseanna dela Mare was married to? Funny he'd still be around. How long did he play with the Red Sox? Do we know?"

"Six years more or less, according to the Sox publicity office. They told me where Kirby was. Seems they keep tabs on their old-timers." He drank from his coffee cup and sighed. "But maybe Kirby and Roseanna didn't keep in touch with each other after all this time. Still, you never know . . ." He sighed again and seemed lost in thought.

She drained her cup. "I'm ready whenever you are, Chief."

"Uhmmm," he grunted and reached for his jacket. He seems a little better, she thought, more with it.

The Kirby house was a classic farmhouse: two-story white clapboard, a wide porch across the front and a high peaked tall chimney house drawn by a child.

Knute parked under a big maple so that the shade would keep the car cooler. The July day was so hot he decided to leave his jacket in the car. Officer Buono was in uniform so she couldn't opt for comfort. Then again, why couldn't she? They were out in the country where no one could see; still, she didn't . . . He knocked hard on the frame of the screen door. "Why don't you take off your jacket?" he was saying when they heard footsteps.

The man who approached them was square in silhouette and as he came nearer, Knute could see that he was fat. He looked, thought Knute, like a Buddha in blue jeans. "Mr. Kirby," he said when only the screen door separated them, "we're police officers from Wellesley. May we have a few words with you?"

"Sure. Come on in." Kirby pushed the door aside so that they could enter. They followed him through the hall to the kitchen, a farm kitchen with a pine table, a linoleum floor and an old-fashioned black iron stove. It was, somewhat unexpectedly, spotlessly clean.

"Have a seat," said Kirby, pushing a chair out for Alice Buono. "Can I get you a cup of coffee? I got Kava instant. No acid in it. My gut can't take the caffeine acid anymore but since I'm a member in good standing with AA I got to drink something."

"Yes, thank you." Alice smiled up at him. "Black, please. No sugar."

"You know of the death of Roseanna dela Mare?" Knute couldn't imagine that Kirby hadn't heard of it. The media had told the story at length and in great detail.

Kirby, tending to a boiling kettle on the stove, had his back to them. "I was at the funeral," he said. He came to the table with filled mugs. "I hadn't seen her for almost twenty years. There's nothing I can tell you about her. I didn't know anything about any Roseanna dela Mare. It was Roseanna Randolph that I knew." He pulled up a chair between the two of them. "That's the only reason I went to the funeral, for Roseanna Randolph. Damned lousy way to die. Especially Roseanna. She hated the cold." He drank from the coffee cup, which concealed his face for a moment. "How'd you find out about me?" he murmured. "I thought it was all forgotten."

"She wrote about it." Knute wondered why Kirby was being so defensive. If he'd had no contact with his ex-wife in twenty years he should have nothing to hide.

Kirby looked directly at Knute. Close up, Knute could see that his eyes were brown with blue circles at the edges. Cataracts? Knute wasn't sure. Kirby asked, "She wrote about me?"

"She wrote about her girlhood. We followed it up."

"What did she have to say about me?"

"Only that she had married this nice young baseball player," Alice answered quickly. "She didn't get any further than that."

"Oh." He's disappointed, thought Knute. He was hoping for more, some nostalgic words on a lost romance. Something along the lines of "I'm so sorry I let him go . . ."

"How long were you married?"

"To Roseanna?" He smiled with pride. "I've had five wives, you know. Never had any trouble getting the ladies to say yes." He laughed harshly. "Never had no trouble getting rid of them either."

"So how long were you married to Roseanna?"

He grimaced. "Not long. Not long but it seemed like . . . She was my first sweetie, you know." He gave Knute a man-to-man look. "You know how it is with the first one. Kid stuff, but the first time . . ." He frowned. "We were married a little over a year. For one thing, she didn't like all the traveling. Then, too, some of the ballplayers were pretty rough in those days. No college boys then. And she didn't feel at home in Boston." He grunted. "Yet that's where she ended up. Life's funny, ain't it?

Guess she learned to feel at home. Maybe when she had enough money she learned to feel at home. I still don't see why you'd come out here to talk to me. There ain't nothin' I can tell you and I got work to do. Just broke for lunch, that's all. That's the only reason you've found me here in the middle of the day."

"The tragedy at the picnic—we wanted to know about that." Alice took up the conversation. "It was a horrible thing—she must have been devastated. Especially since she was so young."

"God almighty, yes. It was awful. We'd just got started when we had to come back. I thought she'd kill herself from crying. I never saw anybody cry so long or so hard. The doc had to knock her out. It was awful. She kept sayin' if only she had been there. I told her that was nuts. If she'd been there she'd be gone, too, but she said no, she could have stopped them, she'd have saved them. And then she'd cry."

"What did she mean by that, that she would have saved them?" asked Knute.

"She was just crazy with grief, that's all. Roseanna was smart, probably the smartest girl I ever knew, but she wasn't smart enough to know the lemonade was spiked with poison. I don't think she was that smart."

"Did they ever figure out how it happened?"

"They said it was just an accident. They said they'd never find out how the poison got into the kitchen because anybody who could have told them was dead. They told me I got to help Roseanna forget it and I tried." He slapped the table. "God knows I tried." He shook his head. "Funny thing was, when she finally stopped crying I never saw her shed a tear again. It was like she was all cried out, for all time." He looked to each of them. "You figure that happening did something to her head way back then? Something that caused her to kill herself all this time later?"

Knute shook his head. He didn't know exactly what he wanted to ask Kirby next. He didn't even know why he'd driven out here. Just to keep busy, to have something to do, to be young Detective Knute Severson again instead of the aging chief, maybe. What could Fred Kirby know about a rich woman who'd meant nothing to him in years . . . "You said you'd seen her twenty years ago. What was the occasion?"

"Yeah, it was twenty years ago. Well, maybe not quite twenty. It was in the late sixties. We got together for a little 'remember when' session. Actually, I was in the hospital and she came to see me. You could have knocked me over with a feather when she came into the ward. All dolled up, she was, looked like a million bucks. God, was I ever born before my time! If I'd've played ball these days I could have ended up with a sackful of dough. You know how much they paid in those days? Unless you was Babe Ruth or Lou Gehrig, one of those guys, all you got was peanuts. I wouldn't have had to go begging to Roseanna to buy this farm if things was different then. I was every bit as good as Brooks Robinson, you know. I got clippings—"

"Mrs. dela Mare gave you the money to buy this farm?"

Kirby got up and went back to the stove. "I didn't say she gave me the money. More like she loaned it to me."

"Did you pay her back?"

He turned, angry. "I'm workin' on it." He realized what he'd said. *"Was* working on it. It takes time, you know, to come back when you get to be my age. I had to learn like a baby, to stay sober, watch my health, keep the house, plow and plant. It takes time!"

"I'd say you've done very well," Alice spoke softly. "It couldn't have been easy."

He reacted like a kid who's been patted on the head. "It wasn't. You know it was damned hard. And I'm grateful to her. I don't guess anybody else would have given me the time of day. But she wasn't sweet about it, you know what I mean? She didn't do it like she wanted to but like she had to. That's why I never bothered her no more. Not even to say thank you."

"We'll grab a bite to eat," Knute announced as he drove away from Kirby's place, "and then we'll drive on out to Northampton and visit the former Mrs. Gordon dela Mare. I'll telephone her from a public phone along the way so she'll know we're coming. I wouldn't want to drive all that way for nothing."

"Northampton? We'll be late getting back." She could visualize it now. She'd never be able to meet Brad at seven o'clock and she had no idea how to let him know.

"If it runs into dinnertime, a good meal's on me, okay? And time and a half, of course." He tried a laugh that sounded a little annoyed, Alice thought. "Or did you have important plans for this evening?"

"No, no, that's fine. I'll just call my mom if it looks like we're running late." What else could she say? I've got this date with this hunk . . . silly girls talked that way, not responsible women. Not women who cared about their jobs, who wanted a career in a field that wasn't that easy . . . "I wish Mrs. dela Mare had written more of her autobiography. She's a hard woman to understand."

The chief nodded. "A complex personality. If it weren't for the light bulb outside the freezer I might buy the suicide theory."

"Uhmm, maybe. But she was in good health, had a nice place to live, had friends. I always thought people who took their own lives did so out of despair."

"I guess there's all kinds of despair," said Knute and after that they were silent for a good part of their drive on the Mass. Pike.

Catlin dela Mare was waiting for them in her elegant apartment in what looked to be a brand-new complex. Knute identified himself for the intercom system and was rewarded by the buzzing of the heavy glass door. He pushed it open so that Alice could enter before him and they walked on a thick oriental carpet, looking for apartment numbers.

Mrs. dela Mare's apartment was number 108. She was waiting at the door, a tall, thin woman with red hair. "Has something else happened?" was her greeting. "Is something wrong with Gordon? Please come in and tell me what's the matter." She's a nervous type, thought Alice. She's got something on her mind, thought Knute.

"We're just following up on Mrs. dela Mare's death," he assured her. The woman really looked frightened. Of what? "So far as we know, your husband is quite all right."

"My ex-husband," corrected Catlin dela Mare. "Please sit down. Victoria is away at school so we can talk freely. I don't like to discuss her grandmother's passing in her presence. Young people take such things to heart, you know. Can I get you some coffee?"

"No," Knute spoke quickly; he'd had enough coffee. "No, thank you. We won't take much of your time. We're just looking into the background of Mrs. dela Mare, trying to get a handle on her personality. We've just seen her first husband and now we're here to talk to you. I don't know if you realize she had a first husband. What we're doing is a little like trying to fit a jigsaw puzzle together."

"Oh, I knew about the first husband. A drunken ex-ball-player. I was dating Gordon when they told her he was in the hospital, nearly dead. She flew right to his side. I could never understand why. He sounded perfectly loathsome. We—Gordon and I—thought it must be a case of a guilty conscience."

"A guilty conscience?"

"Because she ran out on him all those years before. We didn't know the story, of course. She told Gordon only that she'd been married before. A youthful mistake, she said, a peccadillo. At any rate, we could imagine . . ." She tried a smile and managed a grimace. "After all, we were in love once. And I can't speak for Gordon but I get guilt feelings every so often." The twitchy smile turned into a brief, bitter laugh.

"What did you think of your mother-in-law? What kind of woman was she?"

She considered the question. "In control. Roseanna was always in control. Or seemed to be. But if she killed herself she must have been seething inside, wouldn't you think?"

Alice had a question. "What about Mr. dela Mare? What sort of man was he? Did they get along well together?"

The smile was broader this time. "Arnold was sweet. He adored Victoria and spoiled her rotten." She looked pensive. "You know, Gordon changed after his father died. I think our marital troubles began then. Victoria's grandfather was—kind of like a cement that held us all together." She clasped her hands in her lap, then squeezed them so tightly they heard a knuckle crack. She looked down in surprise.

"Any theory as to how he died?"

"Why, he drowned, of course. Oh, you mean how did it happen?" She unclasped her hands and put one on each chair arm. "Somehow he knocked himself out, slipped and fell into the sea."

"He was alone, right? No chance of someone else being on the boat with him?"

"No, of course not. How could there be? Everybody knew Roseanna never sailed—she said it made her seasick. There were witnesses at the pier in Hyannisport. He went out alone. Everybody said so. Bill Cullingham was there, he saw him. You know Bill Cullingham, don't you? He's at Shangri-la. He and Arnold were very good friends."

After a moment she pushed herself up from her chair. "Are you sure I can't get you something to drink? Is it too early for a cocktail? Actually, I could use a little pick-me-up myself. Anyone for gin and tonic?"

That's her problem, thought Alice, she drinks. Does Gordon dela Mare know? Surely he wouldn't leave his daughter with her if he knew she had a problem. Unless *he* has a problem.

Catlin dela Mare was making conversation from a cabinet across the way, a cabinet that apparently held her bar supplies. ". . . I know I should go to the memorial service tomorrow but I do hate to take Victoria out of school again."

"Memorial services? For Roseanna dela Mare? Who's planning that?"

"That Mr. Bancroft at Shangri-la, I suppose. It's being held in the chapel there. Miss Evans called me. She said the vacationers are back from Alaska and want to pay their respects. I told her we'd try, I wasn't sure. She said Gordon was going." She turned to face them. "Isn't Gordon enough? Do you think we should go, too? It takes so much out of—Victoria."

Knute rose—a signal to Alice, who also stood. "If it bothers your daughter, I'd say you'd better do what's best for her."

"But what will people say if we aren't there?"

"Maybe," said Knute, "they won't even miss you."

"Do you think she's an alcoholic?" asked Alice as they drove away.

"Maybe. She has some of the signs. I think I should have another session with Gordon dela Mare though, that's what I think. I did him once over lightly and then—everything happened and I never got back to him. Let's see, what time is it? Close to six. Let's go as far as Sturbridge and have dinner there. Then maybe we can tackle Gordon tonight." He looked over at her. "Does that sound okay to you?"

"Yes. Fine. Only . . ."

"Only?"

"I'm not dressed for a nice restaurant. I'd feel funny sitting there in my uniform."

"Don't be silly, you look fine. Just take off your jacket and tie and unbutton your skirt a couple of notches. You'll look like you're wearing a blouse and skirt. Lots of times Brenda . . ." He stopped talking and looked away.

"All right. Yes. I can do that. It's a very good idea. You don't have to really dress for dinner anymore, do you? My mother says girls don't know how to look pretty anymore . . ." She was prattling and she knew it but she had to say something.

And she had to call home as soon as she could. Damn.

After washing up in the men's room, Knute thought it might be a good idea to check in with the station. He'd noticed Alice using one of the pay telephone booths so he went into another. He'd been out of touch all day—there was no radio in his own car. By narrowing his perspective, he could concentrate on one problem. A problem he found interesting, but only clinically interesting . . . "Hello, Bowman. This is Severson. Anything special come up in the last few hours?"

He found Alice sitting at the table when he got back. "We've got to make it quick," he told her. "There's been another one."

"Another?"

"Death at Shangri-la. The Meeny woman, the one in the

wheelchair. She was found at the bottom of the swimming pool. Strapped in her chair."

"Trapped in her chair," Alice amended softly. "Should we skip dinner?"

"No, we've already ordered. I'll just get the waitress to leave the check when she brings the food. What the hell is going on at that place?"

Something very ugly, Alice thought and then the food came.

A little over an hour later Knute drove into the parking area at Shangri-la. The Center was ablaze with lights, and loud voices blended with softer tones to create a babble. Knute and Alice walked through the door and stood there. Heads turned and voices stopped in mid-sentence.

Bancroft and Fancy Evans formed a focal point in front of the fieldstone fireplace. Dozens of well-dressed senior citizens stared at Knute and Alice. It was Alice's uniform that said police.

The voices started up again. "Why weren't we given police protection? That's what I want to know!"

"This security force we pay so much for, it's as useless as tits on a boar hog."

"I'm afraid to step outside my door at night."

"I'm afraid to stay in my house at night. Or in the day!"

"We demand twenty-four-hour police protection. Two of us murdered within ten days!"

"It's a nightmare, I tell you. An absolute nightmare!"

"Who's going to be next?"

Bancroft raised his voice. "This is Chief of Police Severson. I think it might be helpful if you would let him speak."

They closed their mouths and turned toward Knute.

"I've just heard about Mrs. Meeny so I can't tell you anything until I've talked to Mr. Bancroft. If you'll just be a bit patient . . ." He spotted Bill Cullingham and Ward Butler sitting at a card table with two women. Delilah Ventress was in the room, too, tucked into a corner of a big sofa. Also in attendance, rather unexpectedly, was Gary Tate. But then the phys ed man lived on the estate, Knute remembered.

"We demand some answers," a male voice shouted. That started them up again. Knute used his strongest voice. "If you'll just let me confer with Mr. Bancroft, I'll tell you all I can. I've been out of town on this case, and there's nothing I can say until I learn the details."

There was general grumbling and then a female voice said, "That makes sense to me," and on that note Knute and Alice and Bancroft left the room.

"Do you want to talk to Miss Evans?" asked Bancroft as he opened the door to his office.

"Do I need to?" asked Knute.

"She—er—found the body."

"Again?"

"I'm afraid so."

"Alice— Officer Buono, please ask Miss Evans to join us."

Fancy Evans had lost her glow. Her eyes didn't sparkle; even her hair seemed to have lost its shine. "I was taking a shortcut," she told them. "We're supposed to be having this memorial service for Mrs. dela Mare and we've invited a local minister to officiate and I was supposed to meet him at the chapel but I was a little bit late so I took a shortcut through the pool area." She took a deep breath and now her eyes filled with tears.

"I saw this—this darkness in the water at the deep end and I thought, what on earth is that, one of the patio chairs thrown into the pool? I thought maybe some vandals had gotten onto the grounds or the wind had moved it but it hadn't been windy . . . So I went to the side of the pool and looked down and the water kept shifting, and then suddenly Evangeline Meeny was staring up at me!" Her voice caught and she buried her face in her hands.

"She came running for me." Bancroft took up the story. "I went and looked, then called for you fellows. It was obvious there was nothing that could be done. Even so, I had a couple of our security chaps bring her up. I think your lieutenant was a bit miffed about that—disturbing evidence, that sort of thing—but I did it just in case there was any chance at all— There wasn't."

"I never did go to meet Reverend Mitchell," said Fancy Evans morosely. "I forgot all about him. I don't know what he must think."

"They told me she was strapped in her chair. Literally?"

"Yes. The chair was motorized, you see, and it had a strap like an airplane seat. For safety purposes."

"Did she usually go around with the strap fastened?" Knute tried to remember the strap when she'd wheeled suddenly into the kitchen the morning they'd found Roseanna. He couldn't recall it at all.

"No, I don't think so. I'm not sure, I didn't pay that much attention to it but I think I might have noticed if it had been fastened. Don't you think?" Fancy looked to Bancroft for answers.

He rubbed a hand along his jawline. "I never paid much attention either, to tell you the truth. Mrs. Meeny had such a—commanding presence that I never had time to take in the details of her appearance."

"What time of the day did you find the body, Miss Evans?"

"Just past five. I'm certain because I was scheduled to meet Reverend Mitchell at five and, as I said, I was a little late."

"How was it there was no one at the pool? On a hot summer day like this?"

"We traditionally close the pool from four to six," Bancroft told them. "Hendry runs the worm across it then."

"The worm?"

"That's the device that keeps the pool free of falling leaves, debris, silt, that sort of thing. It's a long coil of accordion tubing with some sort of vacuum on the end. Very effective. We call it the worm. Sounds better than snake." He tried to smile.

"And did—what's his name—Henry run the worm this afternoon?"

"Hendry. Yes, he did. About four-thirty, he said. There was, of course, no one in the pool at that time. Nor near the pool. He said it was completely deserted."

"Isn't that a little odd? With all these people milling around the place? Have you asked them? No one saw anything?"

"Your officers were very thorough. But actually that's understandable. We have a routine here. No one set it, it simply evolved. After breakfast one gardens or pursues one's hobbies. After lunch one exercises and naps or naps and exercises. Then one showers and gets ready for the cocktail hour. Then, after dinner, we have cards and/or television in the lounge. You'll find, Chief Severson, that when people reach a certain age they become creatures of habit."

Knute sighed. "We'd like to see Mrs. Meeny's living quarters."

"Shouldn't you say a word to the other residents first?" Bancroft looked anxious. "They are truly concerned."

"Okay. I'll talk to them." So they went out into the lounge again, where Knute made his we're-doing-everything-we-can speech with emphasis on "We have no evidence that the recent deaths at Shangri-la were crimes of violence. I'll admit that it seems a matter for suspicion when you have two sudden deaths in a matter of days, but the possibility remains that both could have been accidental. Or even suicidal."

There was a moment's silence and then a woman's voice said, "Evangeline Meeny was terrified of water." He thought, but couldn't be sure, that the voice had been Delilah Ventress'.

"We'll know more tomorrow when we get a coroner's report," he said. "In the meantime the best thing you can do is follow your regular schedule." Which, I hope, means bed, he thought but didn't add.

"And don't worry," Bancroft appended, "we're in good hands."

The Meeny ménage was furnished with something Alice called early Broyhill. It was cluttered but not unpleasantly so. Knute wondered aloud if Shangri-la provided maid service. Alice thought maids must be available for those who wanted them. Knute told her to make a note: Did Roseanna dela Mare have a maid? Evangeline Meeny?

A lot of TV dinners were in the refrigerator. A jar of jelly beans and a cable TV listing lay on the bedside table. As for cosmetics, a lipstick (Alice reported that the color was Real Red, the brand inexpensive) and a tube of black mascara rested on the vanity table. There was an unopened package, with gold ribbon trim, of cologne with a name that Alice didn't recognize. There was a card tied to the gold ribbon: "Happy Birthday, love, Roger, Cecilia and the kids."

Alice found the *Playgirl* magazines in a desk drawer. There were fifteen of them, all dated a couple of years back. She raised her eyebrows at Knute, flipped a few pages, then put them aside: he thought she blushed.

Underneath the magazines were sheets of paper with writing on them. "Another chapter in the life of Mrs. Meeny," she explained and handed them over.

Knute glanced at the first page. "Tomorrow," he decided. "When I try to read, my eyes cross. What time is it, anyway?"

It was close to midnight when he dropped her off beside her car in the station parking lot. "I'm sorry it's so late," he said.

"That's okay." She dug in her bag for her keys and opened her car door.

"Ah, Buono . . . Alice."

"Yes, sir?" She lifted her head to look at him.

"I just wanted to say— I guess it will sound strange, but I enjoyed today. Getting out of town was a good idea. For me, at least."

She nodded and turned her key in the ignition.

"So, thanks," said Knute.

"You're welcome," said Alice Buono.

Members of the media were waiting for Knute when he arrived at the station the next morning. Newspaper reporters and television crews from all the local papers and stations were there. He had to repeat the question-and-answer sequence three times with three different interrogators and cameramen. No, not all men. One was a female. Each one moved him around, tried for a different effect. He began to feel like an ill-trained actor.

Lieutenant Mark Beavers had a message for him when he finally got away. "Roger Meeny is at his mother's place in Shangri-la. He wants to see you."

"I want to see him. Is Officer Buono in?"

"She's out on school crossing patrol. Harry called in sick." Beavers checked a clipboard. "I think she's over at Schofield if you want to see her."

"It's not necessary. Is Tracy available?"

"Sergeant Tracy is in Needham today. Testifying in the Winslow case."

"Okay. I'll go on my own unless Buono gets back before I leave. I'd like to see your notes from yesterday—I need to go over them before I go out to Shangri-la. If Officer Buono comes in, tell her to see me." And he went into his office to read Lieutenant Beavers' report and the newest Meeny pages.

There was nothing in Beavers' notes that he didn't already know. Lab reports were pending, he needed a medical report and he'd have to question Beavers for more detail about the seat belt of the wheelchair.

Turning to the Meeny pages he read:

Delilah says I ought to tell about Francis. But every time I think about Francis and how he died I get this scary feeling. It's like the world goes black and I've been emptied—everything's gone. Delilah says I've got to write down as much as I remember even though it was so many years ago.

I remember it like it was yesterday.

We'd gone to Lake Belle for our summer vacation. Francis' Uncle George loaned us his cottage for the month of August. Francis got only one week's vacation from his job at the store but he insisted that I take Roger and spend the whole month out there. It was good for the baby *and* for me, he said, and he could come out late Saturdays to spend Sundays with us. It was a long trip, three hours each way, and he didn't get off work until 9 P.M. on Saturdays. He tried to spend as much time as he could with us so he left late on Sunday nights.

You can see it was tiring even though he was young and strong. I often said, "Francis, why don't we come home with you? We don't need to loll around out here while you're at home cooking your own meals and doing your laundry . . ."

But he said it made him feel good to see Roger all golden brown and me looking so rested. He said I deserved to have Mrs. King (who took care of Uncle George's cottage) take care of me, and Roger and I deserved fresh milk and eggs from the farm down the road. He said we only lived once and we should take advantage of every golden opportunity. He talked lots about golden opportunities. He believed in them and that's why he never ever would have committed suicide.

That's what they said he did. How did they know? He drove

home that Sunday night in our nice little Model A and he put the car in the garage and he just sat there because he was so tired. He sat there for only a few minutes. I could see how he'd do that. Well, he fell asleep and the motor was running and he —just—never—woke—up.

I know that's what happened.

I knew *then* that's what happened and I know *now* that's what happened.

I took Roger and went to live with my father, who was a Pentecostal preacher as well as a streetcar conductor. When he told me that Francis had been a sinner who took his own life, a sinner who would wind up in hell, I took Roger and went to live with Francis' mother.

When she tried to have Roger baptized in the Catholic Church I took him and went to live by myself.

I worked at home. I made aprons and pot holders and quilts. I painted china. I knitted sweaters and mittens and caps. I sold them first by standing on street corners, then by knocking on doors. One day I got up enough courage to try selling them to a store. They said they'd pay me less but they'd buy all I could make.

We managed. And when Roger grew up and became a success we had it all.

That's the story of my life.

When Knute got home he saw that the mailbox was stuffed and he realized he'd forgotten to check it since sometime last week. Among the bills and the ads was a letter from Leif. He sat at the kitchen table and opened it.

Dear Dad,

I haven't been feeling very good lately so I went to the camp doctor. He asked me what was wrong and I told him I didn't know, I just felt lousy. So he did some tests and when he was through he said he couldn't find anything physically wrong. So then he said he knew about my mother and he was sorry about that. He thought maybe I was feeling bad because I hadn't taken time to mourn.

I asked him what he meant by that and he said that when something bad happens everybody needs some time to mourn before he can begin to feel better. I thought about that and then I got permission to leave camp for an overnight (I told them I had to go to town on personal business). Then I took my sleeping bag and went up on the mountain, which was kind of a dumb thing to do all alone but I couldn't think of any other place where I could be by myself.

Anyway, I spent the night there and I thought about a lot, mostly about all the good times we had, and I cried some. When I got back to camp I realized that I did feel better so I thought I'd better write you and tell you about the doctor's prescription in case you haven't been feeling good either.

Only two more weeks and I'll be home.

Love, your son

Leif

Knute sat there reading the letter again and again as though he had to memorize it.

After a while he cried a little.

But not enough.

And perhaps for the wrong reasons.

"You're a very difficult young lady to reach." Brad Preston sounded a little on the curt side, Alice thought. No doubt he expected profuse apologies but she wasn't in the mood. She'd done her best to let him know about the broken date; she couldn't help it if her job came first. Wouldn't his job come first if the situation were reversed? You bet it would!

She said offhandedly, "We've been busy lately. We've got a couple of big problems on our hands so we're putting in some overtime."

"I read about your problems in the paper this morning." His voice was lighter now. Debonair—that was the word for him. Like Fred Astaire, only he didn't look anything like Fred Astaire. "Two suspicious deaths at a posh old folks' home in Wellesley. Rare occurrences, the paper intimated."

"Yes. Very."

"And your boss, I saw him on television. A good-looking guy. A little on the over-the-hill side, maybe. Is he hard to work for?"

"No, of course not." She felt defensive and hoped she didn't sound that way. What did he expect a chief of police to be, a teenage wimp?

"Hey, I didn't mean to strike a nerve. No hard feelings? I just wanted to ask you out to dinner. How about tonight?"

She must have taken too long to answer because he went on. "Or, if not tonight, tomorrow night? Look, I'm not going to give up until we get together again. I'm a determined kind of guy."

"I'd like to go. I only hesitated because I never know when

something might come up. Like last time. I really am sorry about that. I couldn't call you. I didn't know how to get in touch with you."

"Hey, I understand. I'm willing to take a chance. And here's my number, write it down. 555-0030. And I take rain checks. Shall we try for tonight?"

Yes, she said. So long as he understood. Yes, he said. He understood. Really. Hanging up she felt that odd mixture of excitement and apprehension that Brad Preston brought on. Why did he find her especially attractive? Perhaps if they went out again she'd find out.

Chief Severson had a meeting set up with Roger Meeny. Evangeline's son had arrived late the previous evening. He'd taken up residence at the Holiday Inn just over the line in Natick. He was expecting them so they went directly to his unit. Knute knocked.

The man who opened the door was balding and heavyset. He wore a dress shirt open at the neck without a tie and a pair of baggy, sky blue pants. The pants were held up by a leather belt with a brass belt buckle. Alice couldn't make out the pattern on the buckle because his stomach obscured the design.

"Come in, Chief, ma'am. You had any coffee this morning? I had room service send in a pot and some extra cups. Just in case. And some croissants. Just in case anybody's hungry. Sit down, will you, and tell me what happened. God, I couldn't believe it when they called me. Ma had the spinal problem but outside of that she was good for years. I thought maybe she'd even live longer than me." He shook his head in obvious sorrow. The hair left on it was reddish, his eyes a washed-out blue.

When Knute agreed to have coffee Alice followed his lead. She'd noticed that the chief had trouble dealing with the bereaved. Her uncle Anthony had told her it was easier when you grew up in a big family—people were dying all the time so you got lots of practice. Her uncle Anthony was a funeral director. Who else knew better about such things?

Now the chief was asking Mr. Meeny, "Would she have committed suicide? For any reason that you could think of?"

"Ma? Never in a million years. If you'd known my mother— Listen, she was the leading optimist in the whole world. She saw everything better than it was. For instance, she was always telling people what a successful man I was. But I'm just an average guy. I've got a food franchise restaurant in a not-so-hot location. And not a McDonald's either—just a third-rate hamburger and ice cream stand and believe me, it takes a lot of work to make it pay for my family, to say *nothing* of keeping Ma up here. This Shangri-la is not cheap, you know. But it's what she wanted. She knew some of these people from way back, see, and she couldn't have stood it if she couldn't have it as good as they did. That's the way she was, my mother. A great kidder, only the only person she kidded was herself. To hear her tell it, I'm rich, my wife's a former Miss America, and my boys are budding geniuses. Mother always had the best, to hear her tell it."

Alice could imagine what the chief was thinking. Did Roger Meeny resent having to pay for his mother's stay at Shangri-la? Enough to have come up here—or even paid somebody—to push his mother into the pool? Knute was asking, "Did she really believe she had the best? That could be a reason, you know. She got tired of putting up a pretense—"

Roger Meeny shook his head vehemently. "She believed. I tell you, she believed. You should hear her go on about my dad, for instance. He was God's gift to women, smart as hell, good, kind, every girl's dream. To hear her tell it, that is. I don't remember him but I've seen pictures of him and talked to people who knew him. Even my grandparents said sure, he was honest and decent and all that, but nothing special. Only she didn't see him that way. Nor me. Nor anybody else she wanted to put on a pedestal."

Chief Severson finished his coffee, then put the cup down. "We have to consider suicide and you say no. We have to consider an accident but we don't think so. We're not certain but we don't think so. So that leaves—"

"Murder? Why would somebody kill my mother?" The pale blue eyes were as wide as they could get. "That's the craziest thing I ever heard. Why? You're way off if you think that."

"It doesn't seem to make much sense, I'll admit that." Knute moved the coffee cup around a little. "Did you have any insurance on her?"

"Insurance? Jesus! All I'm able to afford is a burial policy and maybe that won't even be enough."

Knute pushed back his chair in a sudden movement. "I suppose you can prove where you were yesterday?"

"Me?" Roger stood, too. "Me? Of course I can. I was working my tail off at the restaurant all day. Do you mean you suspect me?"

"It's routine to check on family." Alice scrambled to her feet to follow Knute to the door. "How about your wife and sons?" He threw that in almost as an afterthought.

Now Roger Meeny bristled. "My wife is my cashier in the restaurant. And my boys are in school. You people have got to be sick. Here I do my best, bust my butt to take care of my mother and you put me numero uno on your suspect list! Well, I'll tell you what you can do, Chief Severson—get the hell out of here. If you've got anything else like that to say to me I'm calling a lawyer!"

Knute made a command performance before the Board of Selectmen. He hadn't appeared before the Board since just prior to the last Town Meeting. They'd changed chairmen in the interim and it was Charlie Barnes' turn at the post. Charlie was the newest of the three-person Board. Veteran selectman Ernest Kilmer called him "the ribbon clerk" behind his back. But though Charlie had the looks and manner of a college boy, he was far from that, Knute knew. He was a very successful executive with a computer company on Route 128. Smarter than he seemed.

Because residence in Wellesley was far from cheap and because Wellesley residents had long been members of the upwardly mobile class, the local government drew from a pool of well-educated, civic-minded citizens. In Knute's opinion higher education and lofty ideals didn't necessarily lead to intelligent judgment, but by and large the results were beneficial to the general public. Those who served got little or no money for their efforts. There were perks, of course. A subtle sort of power. A sense of accomplishment. Your name in the *Townsman* every week. No guarantee of public recognition, but a shot at it.

The current board was filled out, in more ways than one, by Ms. Jennifer Cobell, who was a vice president of a prestigious Boston bank. Jenny, as she liked to call herself, appeared to be the state-of-the-art executive of the eighties. In Knute's opinion, she was sharp enough to split hairs endwise and therefore should be approached with caution. On hand, as always, to assist the Board was their executive secretary, Kent Cline.

The Board wanted to talk about the deaths at Shangri-la, but the presence of the press (one from the *Townsman,* two from city papers) inhibited such frank conversation; so the Board went into executive session, thus temporarily eliminating the audience.

"What the heck's going on out there, Chief?" Charlie Barnes' Boston accent made him sound like Ted Kennedy.

"We're investigating two deaths of elderly women." Just the facts, sir, just the facts. "We can't be sure they were accidental."

Jenny Cobell frowned. To her a frown was just a tiny line between her well-arched brows that hardly rippled the porcelainlike surface. "What do you mean, you can't be sure?"

"They look like accidents on the surface. But in each case there was something that wasn't right. You know, like that newspaper cartoon, 'What's Wrong with This Picture?' "

Ernest Kilmer linked his hands, then leaned his chin on them. "And just what was wrong with the picture?"

Knute told them about the safety light over the freezer door, and the seat-belt buckle on the wheelchair.

Jenny Cobell nibbled daintily on the end of her note-taking pen. "That hardly seems conclusive. Perhaps the light bulb just wasn't installed properly. As for the seat belt, perhaps she just couldn't undo it."

"Or maybe she just plain committed suicide," Charlie interjected.

Knute shrugged. "So far as we can determine, the light was in working order. The bulb, however, hadn't been screwed tightly enough. And Evangeline Meeny wasn't the type to kill herself . . . there are usually signs when a person's contemplating suicide, and she just didn't fit the profile."

"You know the publicity on this is beginning to make the town look bad." Ernest Kilmer was probably the most visible of the selectmen, usually managing to appear in at least three pictures in each week's *Townsman:* one for ribbon cutting, one for some sort of charity drive and one for something social at the country club.

"I don't like it any better than you do," Knute told them. "I don't think they would have paid as much attention if the first victim hadn't been the dela Mare woman. That made them prick up their ears and then when this second death occurred . . . Well, I just don't know how to handle them. Maybe you've got some ideas."

"It seems to me the most sensible thing is for you to simply declare the deaths accident and suicide, and then let it go at that," Ms. Cobell said.

"I don't think I could do that." Knute realized his teeth were on edge and he eased his jaw.

"You don't see how you could do that, hmmm?" Charlie Barnes had wide, unblinking blue eyes. Knute wondered fleetingly how he'd managed to keep that innocent look.

"No, I don't. I think I ought to look around some more. Then if I don't find anything I'll drop the whole business. But, right now . . ." He shrugged. "I just feel like there's something funny there."

"These are wealthy people." Jenny Cobell stared into space over his head. "They've been prominent in their day, most of them, and some are still influential. I've had several phone calls . . ."

Knute didn't say anything.

"By the way"—Charlie filled in the pause—"did you happen to see the figures from the latest FBI *Uniform Crime Reports?* They were in the paper the other day. There was a map on the incidence of murder in the U.S.; Massachusetts rated pretty well with only 3.5 percent."

"Who had the fewest?" Ernest wanted to know.

"North Dakota, I believe. Only 1 percent. And the highest was Texas. I felt pretty good about our showing. The average for the U.S. was 8 percent." Charlie shook his head. "As nations go, that's pretty high."

"It's all those handguns," Jenny Cobell declared.

"And immigrants," Ernest grunted.

"But Wellesley has an extremely good record in that statistical area." Charlie smiled at Knute, white teeth in a tan face. "And we're hoping to keep it that way. I know Chief Severson does his very best—"

"I think you'd better keep us up to date on this Shangri-la situation." Jenny looked directly at Knute now. "Check in with Kent on a daily basis, please. We can't have this sort of thing getting out of hand."

"I may run over there to see for myself." Ernest checked his date book. "I've got a little time tomorrow—"

"Thank you for coming in, Chief." Charlie rose and put out his hand across the table. Knute stood up and obediently shook it, then turned to go.

"Oh, and Chief . . ."

"Yes."

Charlie Barnes put on a very solemn expression. "I'm very sorry about your recent bereavement."

"Yes, indeed," murmured Jenny Cobell.

"A tragic thing." Ernest Kilmer shook his head. "Very tragic."

Knute didn't answer.

Brad took Alice to a restaurant called Finally Michael's, located two towns west in Framingham Center. The interior walls and partitions were shelved and filled with old books. She liked that. She felt as though she were dining in a library. The books nearest her elbow were by S. S. Van Dine. *The "Canary" Murder Case, The Gracie Allen Murder Case.* Old mysteries. She'd like to read them, maybe at the Wellesley Free Library . . .

"Hey! Talk to me." Brad, smiling, reached out and took her hand. "When you grow up, we'll get you a library card."

"I like this place. I've never been here before."

"I should have asked. What are your favorite restaurants?"

"Oh, Ken's. Everybody loves Ken's, I guess. I've been going there for years. My folks used to take us when we were old enough to behave. And Marconi's. Do you know Marconi's? In Ashland? It's Italian."

He grinned. "I always check with the natives to find out where they eat. I had a hunch you'd know the best Italian restaurant."

"Just because my name is Buono doesn't mean we eat nothing but pasta. My father is fourth-generation American and my mother's family goes back to Ireland and the potato famine."

"Was I being patronizing? Sorry." He looked down at the table and played with his fork. "To tell you the truth, you intimidate me. Just a little." He looked up at her and smiled. "I've known a lot of pretty women all over the world but I've never dated a lady policeman who's spent her entire life in Wellesley, Massachusetts."

"You make me sound like Gidget in uniform." Somehow, when he was trying to be his nicest he was his most irritating. He realized it, too, and sobered.

"See what I mean?" he asked. "I'm not making Brownie points, am I? Listen, when we're through here let's go someplace where there's music, some slow dancing, maybe a mirrored globe that whirls around on the ceiling. Atmosphere! I need all the help I can get."

She had to laugh. "That sounds great but I don't know where we'll find that make-believe ballroom."

"Maybe there isn't one. But I do know a place that's on the romantic side. Have you ever been to Bebe's? No? Well, you'll like it, I think. Just trust me." The waiter came then with the check and Brad proffered his credit card, which the waiter bore away. Alice asked to be excused and went to the ladies' room.

When she returned, hair combed and lipstick freshened, Brad escorted her out. He was saying something but she really wasn't listening. She was wondering about the woman she'd just seen Chief Severson with and what in the world he was doing with her at Finally Michael's with his wife dead only weeks ago.

Who, wondered Knute, was the man escorting Alice Buono out of the restaurant? She was about the last person he'd expected to see at Finally Michael's. Good thing she hadn't seen him. He didn't need any faintly accusatory glances from co-workers; he felt guilty enough as it was. But, damn it, he'd felt the need for company and he'd run into Linda Maynard at the Star Market—literally *run* into her coming out of an aisle near the frozen food section.

She smiled across the table now. She looked like what she was—an attractive, middle-aged, exceptionally successful realtor. Knute had met her when she'd showed him the house on Howe Street. That was over sixteen years ago. Just before Leif was born. Knute had never encountered Mr. Maynard. The theory was that she'd divorced him not too long after marrying him, but nobody seemed to really know. Linda Maynard was not prone to personal confessions. Probably that was why he'd asked her out. No complications.

He picked up a conversation they'd begun earlier. "The house is a mess. I didn't realize it,—hell, I didn't even *see* it until I began to think about Leif coming home at the end of next week. I don't know how we're going to manage. I can stick a frozen dinner in the oven—just barely—but we can't eat packaged foods all the time. Then there's the laundry. Sure, we've got a washer and dryer but some clothes have got to be ironed and then there's folding and putting away—somebody's got to do that, and as for dusting and vacuuming . . ."

"I've got at least a partial solution for you, Knute." Linda's short red hair gleamed in the soft light. "You need help in the worst way so I recommend the worst way cleaners . . . Oh, Knute, forgive me. I couldn't resist making that very bad joke. But seriously I recommend the In-House Cleaners. I use them myself, they're very efficient, trustworthy, not overly expensive . . ."

"Do they come every day?"

"I have them once a week. They'll come as often as you need them if they take you on. They can do a lot in five hours. There are two of them, they work in tandem. Here's the number— why not call for an interview? I took it upon myself to recommend you so they'll be expecting your call."

"You've recommended me? You must be clairvoyant."

She laughed. "I called after we chatted at the market. You looked so helpless I checked to see if they had any time. One customer has just moved away so I think you're in unless you scare them off. Now, what's for dinner? You know, I'm hungry for lobster, I haven't had any in ages."

She asked only one question about the deaths at Shangri-la ("Anything new?") and then spent the rest of the evening telling him sometimes sad, occasionally boring and often funny tales of houses sold and left unsold. She was pleasant company, he decided, but no spark there at all, no temptation. Maybe he'd ask her out again.

He had to be at home when the In-House Cleaners arrived but eventually he'd give them a key, if they suited him, that is. So he lingered over coffee two mornings later and was gratified when the doorbell rang exactly at 9 A.M., as advertised.

Standing on the front porch when he opened the door were two tall young ladies, looking exactly alike; both had long, silver-blond hair. One had a baby in a pack attached to the front of her whereas the other held a fair-haired toddler by the hand.

"Yes," said Knute, taken aback, "what can I do for you?"

"We're the In-House Cleaners," the one with the toddler answered him. "I'm Ingrid."

"I'm Inge," said the other. A tiny frown marred the perfect forehead. "You were expecting us?"

"Yes. Sure. Come on in."

Behind them they pulled, each with a free hand, a cartlike arrangement that turned out to contain cleaning tools of all descriptions and a fold-out playpen, which they quickly set up in the living room. Into the pen went baby and small child; the women donned aprons, announced they were ready and asked what he wanted done.

General cleaning. Washing. Ironing. Everything was in a mess. Could they do it all in one day? he wondered. He tried not to let his doubts show. They didn't look anything like house-cleaners and furthermore, who went out to work with tiny children in tow?

"We'll be through by two, I should imagine," said Inge—or was it Ingrid? "If you'll show us where the washer and dryer is . . ."

He showed them through the house, located the clothes hamper (overflowing), gave general directions and fled. He'd felt extremely uncomfortable leaving strangers in his house and yet what else could he do? He went to work and found Fancy Evans waiting to see him.

"I've got a bone to pick with you." She sounded like a heroine in a classic novel, Knute thought. She even looked like one, too, in a lacy dress with matching hat. Women's fashions! He'd never been able to keep up with them. Newspaper ads showed petticoats and ruffles, shades of his school days, pre-jeans and pre–pink punk hair.

"What can I do for you, Miss Evans?"

"Delilah, Miss Ventress that is, told me you'd been reading everyone's autobiographies for clues." She pouted prettily. "But you didn't ask for mine." She took a manila envelope from her lap and placed it on his desk. "So I brought it anyway. I wrote a lot about Shangri-la." She leaned forward. "You never know—I may have seen something significant but didn't know it . . . in the mystery books I've read, that happens all the time. Someone sees something without realizing its importance." She pushed the envelope at him. "So here."

What else could he say but "Thank you"?

"I made copies so you don't have to return these pages." She pushed her chair back and stood up. "We're very anxious to end this dreadful business, you know. The residents are edgy. Mr. Bancroft says he'd appreciate anything you could do to hurry things along, so I'm just doing anything *I* can to facilitate your findings." She put out her hand. "Thank you very much, Chief Severson. Let me know if there's anything else I can do."

"I'll do that, Miss Evans," he said gravely. "I'll get in touch with you right away just as soon as I come to any conclusion."

Bemused, he sat back at his desk when she'd gone and opened the envelope. The pages were perfectly typed. Not surprising, Knute thought. That's the way she'd do things.

He read. "Right the First Time" by Fancy Elizabeth Evans.

My mother always said if you do things right the first time you'll never have to do them over or feel guilty about doing them wrong. For this reason, I have always tried to do things right the first time, even though it's not always easy.

My mother was a very unusual woman. She taught dancing—tap, modern and ballet. I was a big disappointment to her, she said, because I had two left feet. But not to worry, she said, I was pretty and I did learn good posture. And how to walk gracefully.

My mother and father were divorced. She said he used to beat her and she wouldn't stand for that. He was supposed to send her money for child support but he never did. Or hardly ever did. I think she rather liked it that he didn't send her any money. It gave her something to complain about. Or to *not* complain about. Nobly. As I said, my mother was an unusual woman.

She never let up. She was on top of me all the way. I had to get good grades; I had to get a college scholarship. So I did. I always did what she told me to do. Right the first time.

I went into social work. Doing things for other people. Since I'm not at all creative, it was my next choice. I found I liked doing things for other people. I'm not sure Mother thought I'd chosen wisely. I think she would have preferred something more lucrative but she said she did understand the satisfaction I must get from my work.

But there is a problem. I have a tendency to get too emotionally involved with those who depend on me. I had to change that; I even underwent therapy for a while to correct it. But it all got straightened out when I came to Shangri-la to work with Mr. Bancroft. I found that here I can keep my emotional distance and still be of assistance. I'm pretty sure I can.

Not that I am uncaring. I have many favorites at Shangri-la; that's only human. The thing is, I no longer let those likes and dislikes influence my judgment.

Take Mr. Cullingham, for instance. I feel so sorry for that man. All alone. I think his only friends are at Shangri-la—there just isn't anybody else. He was married at one time, according to the records. But his wife died and there's no other family at all. I don't know how she died. Mr. Bancroft said it wasn't the sort of thing one asked if one were at all sensitive. I understood, so naturally I've never brought it up. Even though I *am* curious. I do feel so sorry for him.

Now, Mr. Butler, he's just the opposite so far as I can tell. He is COLD. Mrs. Butler is much more friendly. She likes to party and have fun, and she has this nice sense of humor. She laughs at just about anything. Mr. Bancroft said she swallowed a giggle feather.

But Mr. Butler! No matter how nicely I say good morning, he just sort of mumbles back at me. And it's not just me. It's almost everybody. The only person I ever saw him smile at was the pool boy. And I certainly don't know why. Eugene isn't at all good-looking and he certainly isn't very bright. I hate to say this, but could it be possible that Mr. Butler has a thing for young boys? Mr. Bancroft says of course not, don't even *think* such things. But I do think such things sometimes because I just can't see why Mr. Butler would waste a smile on Eugene, the pool boy.

Friendliness is so important, isn't it? I do try always to be friendly and helpful—it's just my nature. That's another thing my mother taught me. Good manners! Mrs. dela Mare has beautiful manners but Mrs. Meeny—well, Mr. Bancroft describes her as being very down-to-earth. I'd say so! Just a nice way of saying coarse. She just doesn't have any tact. She doesn't have any friends that I know of, and her son that she's always bragging about, well, he isn't so much. There were even times when he got behind in his payments for Mrs. Meeny. I once asked Mr. Bancroft what he'd do if Mrs. Meeny's son got too far behind in his payments; would he ask Mrs. Meeny to leave? Mr. Bancroft said he certainly hoped that would never happen because he would be very loath to evict the poor old girl. Those were his very words. He's such a caring person, Mr. Bancroft.

He got the call at home, early, even before he'd had his coffee. The selectmen wanted him at Town Hall. Pronto. They had something they wanted him to see. Kent wasn't even particularly polite about it.

SODOM, GOMORRAH AND WELLESLEY? That was printed kitty-corner across the cover of a publication called *International Interviewer*. Knute figured that was as close as the rag could get to *National Enquirer* without being sued. He'd seen the magazine before, tucked in alongside its tacky relatives on the supermarket checkout racks. He'd seen people surreptitiously reading it while standing in line, putting it back, not buying it. He'd noted headlines like DEAD WOMAN DELIVERS LIVE BABY and DID VANNA WHITE GET HER GOOD LOOKS FROM OUTER SPACE GODMOTHER? This issue was introduced as being PART ONE OF OUR NEW SERIES—DANTE'S INFERNO TODAY—WHERE TO GO, WHO TO SEE!

Inside he read on: SNOBBY WELLESLEY SCENE OF DRUGS, DEATH, DEVILISH DOINGS. He looked up at the selectmen. "What do you want me to do? Arrest somebody?"

"I take it you haven't read it?" Jenny Cobell looked ready to go to war.

He shook his head. "It's not on my subscription list." He knew he sounded snide but she affected him that way, and right at this moment he didn't particularly care.

"Better look it over." Ernest Kilmer, usually unflappable, sounded almost tense.

Knute read on. *"Peyton Place* has nothing on Wellesley, Massachusetts, a town that could use as its motto 'Isn't it sad that we're better than you are?' " the story began. He started scanning the paragraphs, slowed his pace and then began to read carefully. The three selectmen and their executive secretary made no sound until he'd finished.

"Well?" asked Charlie Barnes.

Knute watched his hand crumple the pages, release them and then crumple them again. Somewhat to his surprise he found his mouth still worked and his voice carried.

"Some of it's lies. The rest of it, well, they make it sound a lot worse than it is. Somebody told them this—somebody who knows which closet doors to open. I don't know what or why or who but they've turned it into garbage."

Jenny Cobell raised elegant eyebrows. "Someone in the police department? Much of it reads almost as though it comes from the police blotter."

Knute took a deep breath. "It could be." It could be someone from this room, too, he thought.

"Any idea who?" asked Ernest.

Knute shook his head. He had no idea. No idea at all.

"Kent, you got in touch with town counsel. Can we sue these bastards? Excuse me, Jenny." Charlie Barnes gave her a quick, boyish smile, turned it off. "Can we sue these sons of guns?"

Jenny raised her eyebrows. "Sons of guns?"

The executive secretary shook his head. "He hadn't seen it. He doesn't have an opinion yet. He has to study it. You know how careful he is."

Charlie snorted. "Careful? That's an understatement!"

"Oh, for heaven's sake, Charlie." Jenny sighed, trying to remain patient. "The man has to read the article before he can offer an opinion."

"Let me see that thing." Ernest reached for the magazine.

"Who is this Bradford Preston? 'By Bradford Preston,' it says. Anybody ever heard of him?"

"I'll find out," Knute promised. He pushed his chair back. He had to get out of there.

"Keep in touch, close touch," Ernest told him. "A lot of people are going to be burned over this."

Knute nodded and started for the door.

"Chief Severson." Jenny called him back.

"Yes?"

"You'd better take this." She pushed the publication toward him. "I don't imagine you'll want to go out and buy one."

"That's an idea." Charlie was excited. "You can send your men to all the markets and pull them off the shelves."

"I don't think—" Kent began.

"Really, Charlie." Jenny Cobell could make you sound like an idiot with only two words.

Knute took the magazine, muttered thanks and hurried out to his car. One paragraph was etched in his brain—just a few sentences he'd never forget.

"The wife of a high muckety-muck in one of the town's most sensitive departments was killed recently in an auto accident. Her highly respected male companion met the same fate. He was driving her back from a weekend on Cape Cod. The registry of the motel where they stayed listed them as Mr. and Mrs. but, of course, they were not married to each other. They were said to be attending a district meeting of library trustees, which, of course, they were not. Yet the local newspaper carried only separate and decorous obituaries with nary a hint of the implications involved, and no one talks publicly about it. That's the way it is in Wellesley. Hush-hush. Garry Trudeau would have a ball."

He crumpled the pages between his hands. He wanted to tear them to pieces.

Leif was coming home in two days. How could he keep him from reading this crap? How could he keep him from finding out?

All the telephone lines were busy when Knute walked into the office. All of the calls, it seemed, were for him.

Andrea Beasley: "Have you seen that filthy rag—what's the name of it, *International Interviewer?* Did you see what it says about me? 'The only son of Congresswoman Andrea Beasley was arrested by local police for possession of a controlled substance, i.e., cocaine, last year. Was young Beasley ever formally charged in Dedham District Court? He was not. Why? Lack of evidence. Really? Says who?' How could that slime sheet find out about Darryl? From someone in your department, that's how. You know he wasn't guilty!"

Harrison Glover: "Where he refers to 'a prominent stockbroker who was kicked out of the country club recently for a rather picturesque crime. Terribly, terribly British and all that, cheating at cards. "Kicked out" isn't how they put it at the club. He was "permitted to resign," which he did prior to tossing back his mane of silver hair and flouncing angrily out.' Don't you know everybody will jump to the conclusion that that's me? Just because my hair is luxuriant and I did resign from the club! For another reason entirely, though—to protest racial and religious discrimination! Now, if they call you in for advice in the situation referred to, you've got to announce that Harrison Glover was not the man involved. My reputation, my very livelihood depends on trust. How can anyone trust a card shark?"

Burford Peeler: "You're gonna get it, you know that. I'm gonna slap you and your department with a lawsuit like you never saw before. That rag practically accuses me of molestation. Just because I carry a few adult features for a special clientele. I do not, and never did, have special filmings in a back room for high school kids. Never! I'm gonna get you for this, Severson, just you wait and see!"

Fancy Evans: "Please, Chief Severson, come at once. There's been another one."

It seemed Ward Butler had shot himself. He was dead in his den—a room, Fancy Evans told Knute, that most of the villagers used as a guest room, but that had been taken over by Mr. Butler as his own. She'd babbled all the way to the Butler cottage and finally shut up only when Bancroft told her to—an action that surprised Knute and Miss Evans and probably Bancroft himself.

Knute had brought Beavers along and had ridden with him in the black Chrysler because it was easier that way. He didn't have the energy to argue with anyone and all he needed to make his day was another Shangri-la body.

Butler lay slumped over a rolltop desk. He'd shot himself in the throat, the bullet passing out the back of the head. The weapon had fallen to the floor. It was a .32 caliber pistol. There were no notes, but a can of gun oil, a box of bullets and what appeared to be a cleaning cloth occupied one corner of the desk top. "The old I-was-only-cleaning-my-gun accident," commented Beavers.

"Looks that way," said Knute.

He had been cleaning his gun, Mrs. Butler told them. She sat despondently on a blue velvet sofa in the living room. A box of tissues on an end table beside her came into good use. On her other side sat Delilah Ventress, who rhythmically patted the widow's hand while murmuring sympathetic sounds.

"He was cleaning his gun because he and Bill were going

hunting as soon as the hunting season opened." Her faded blue eyes filled and she searched for yet another tissue.

"Bill?"

"Bill Cullingham," the Ventress woman answered while patting Amanda Butler's hand.

"What did they plan to hunt?" Knute was truly curious. "Usually hunters carry shotguns."

Her eyes spilled some of their tears. "I don't know. He didn't say. He just said they were going hunting next month so he had to get things in order. He was a very orderly man." She made a moaning noise and buried her face in the tissue.

"Were you in the room when it happened?"

She shuddered and shook her head no.

"Where were you?"

Miss Ventress spoke up. "She's very upset. Can't these questions wait until later? She was here in the living room, doing her crossword puzzle. She does the puzzle in the paper every morning, don't you, dear?"

The bowed head nodded; sobbing sounds came through the tissue.

"Mrs. Butler, I called Dr. Guinness before I left the office." Bancroft looked even more harassed than usual. "She said she'd be right along. She'll give you something, I'm sure . . ." He turned to Knute. "She can look over the body for you, Chief."

Mrs. Butler wailed.

"Doc Bell is on his way," Knute muttered. He'd expected more from Bancroft. After all, the man was responsible for this place . . . Knute felt a sudden urge to sit down. Something was wrong, something inside him; he wasn't feeling very well.

"He'd had his swim, saw to his dahlias." Mrs. Butler had regained some control and was reciting her husband's movements but Knute wasn't listening. A pain from somewhere . . .

a stabbing, grinding, roaring pain hit Knute's left arm, then his shoulder, his chest and his head . . . he couldn't bear it, he was leaving, fading into blackness, he was gone.

The walls of the room were a pale color. There was a window with vertical blinds of the same color and there was a door. He noted these facts before closing his eyes again. When he next opened them he saw that the pale color was a soft green, sort of soothing; there was a blank-faced television attached to a ceiling corner and he was lying in a high bed. He was attached by wire to some kind of machine. He was in a hospital bed. Now he remembered. He'd passed out from the pain. My God, the pain! He wanted to speak, to ask where the pain had come from, where it had gone; questions, he wanted answers to questions. There was a buzzer on a cord lying near his pillow. He pushed at it. Weakly. No one came. He did better the next time.

The nurse was young, red-haired and freckle-nosed. "Well, hello there! A lot of people will be glad to see you're back with us." She automatically reached for a wrist and looked beyond him. He tried to follow her glance but he was caught up in attachments.

"What happened to me?" he asked. "A heart attack? Is that what happened?"

She patted his hand. "Something like that. Dr. Guinness will be in soon, she'll tell you all about it. Or maybe Dr. Bell, they both brought you in." She beamed at him. "You must be really special to have two doctors on your case."

"Where am I? The Newton-Wellesley Hospital?" All he could see out the window were sky and the top of a tree.

"You know it. Our newest intensive care unit. Want a drink of water? Something else?"

"The bathroom. Can I . . ."

"I'll get you a bottle. Can't have you running around until the doctor says so. Meanwhile, there's a young man outside who's been pretty anxious . . ."

"Leif? Is Leif here?"

She grinned, a gamin grin. "I'll send him in."

Knute watched his son push the door open and peer in. How young he looked, how vulnerable. His sandy hair was shaped in what Knute called a tall crew cut but what the kids called it, he didn't know. He liked it, though. It looked like old times . . .

"Dad." Leif came up to the bed, walking quietly and speaking softly to the invalid. "Are you okay? How do you feel? Does anything hurt?"

"I'm okay, Leif. I'm fine. How did you get here? Did somebody go get you?"

"Lieutenant Beavers came. Last night." He put his big hand on Knute's. "Dad, he scared me to death. He didn't mean to, but he did." An attempt at a grin. "I'm too young to be an orphan."

"Sit down. Sit down. There's a chair in the corner, isn't there? Drag it over, sit down. I just had a spell. I don't think it was anything too serious. Well, you can see I'm still kicking. I don't know all the facts myself, the doctor's not been in to tell me. God, I'm glad to see you, Leif . . ."

The red-haired nurse reappeared. She was pushing a cart that held several containers of flowers. "I'm turning this place into a flower shop," she said. She reached under the cart and handed Knute a towel-draped object. "Can you handle this on your own? Want the curtains pulled?"

"I'll help with the flowers," said Leif, turning his back. "Gosh, here's a big bunch—it says they're from the Board of Selectmen. That shows you really rate, doesn't it, Dad? Want me to see who the others are from? 'Everybody at the station,' this one says. I don't know what kind of flowers they are, but there's a lot of them . . ."

"There, that wasn't too difficult, was it?" the nurse asked Knute as she took the towel-draped bottle away. At the door she turned. "I expect the doctor will be in shortly."

"Leif, I'm hooked up to something over my head. What is it? I can't see what it is."

"I don't know what you call it but it looks like one of those things in the movies, you know, those machines that register heartbeats." He came back to the bed. "Lieutenant Beavers said you had a heart attack."

"Yes, I guess I did."

"He said there were doctors right there and they got you an ambulance right away and that's what saved your life."

"I guess it was."

"Oh, Dad." His voice rose like a little boy's. "You've got to be careful!"

"I will, Leif. I will."

The door opened and a doctor appeared. It was Dr. Guinness. Wearing a white coat, she looked like a doctor. She hadn't before, not when Knute had interviewed her. She'd looked more like an actress playing a doctor role.

"Good morning, Chief Severson. How are you feeling today?" Crisp, businesslike tones for medical platitudes. Yes, ma'am, very much the medico. Okay. He'd be very much the macho.

"Okay, I think. Not my usual, but okay. Dr. Guinness, this is my son, Leif."

"Good morning, Leif. I'm going to be doing a little testing on your father for a few minutes. Do you think you could wait outside while I'm doing that? I won't be long."

Leif looked doubtful. "Yeah. Sure." The door closed softly behind him.

"Dr. Bell should be here shortly." Dr. Guinness applied her stethoscope and kept her glance above his head, reading, he supposed, a machine that said he was alive . . . She straightened up. "He's bringing Dr. Bascomb. Perhaps you've heard of him—he's a big heart man at Mass. General."

"It's something bad, then. Something serious." What would happen to Leif if anything happened to him? His mother and father would take over? But they were getting old . . .

Dr. Guinness pulled up a chair and sat on it. "Let's talk about hearts," she said matter-of-factly. "Your heart muscle needs a constant flow of blood because the blood brings oxygen and nutrients necessary for all body organs. Blood reaches your heart through two main coronary arteries. When fatty deposits form in your arteries we call the consequent narrowing of the arteries arteriosclerosis. We think that's your problem, but we need to do more testing before we have a better idea of the extent of the arteriosclerosis. That's where Dr. Bascomb comes into the picture." She smiled brightly. "Don't let all this depress you. You're already one up. You've had a heart attack and you've survived. Now we can help you."

He closed his eyes. The whole world had really turned to crap. "An invalid for the rest of my life, that's . . ." He shook his head to finish the sentence.

"Nonsense." She wagged a finger at him. "Your attack was a minor one, or so we suspect. Therefore you'll be out of bed in forty-eight hours. And even if it is more serious, you'll be permitted to move around to some extent because a certain amount of mobility reduces the risk of a thrombus—that is, a blood clot. And when you get out of here you mustn't even *think* invalid. Damaged hearts heal, just as fractured bones heal. As a matter of fact, ten years after a coronary thrombosis attack your life expectancy will be the same as if you'd never had an attack."

"Ten years? Yeah. Great. Thanks." If he lived that long . . .

Two white coats came through the door. Dr. Bell and Dr. Bascomb, he presumed. Dr. Bascomb was tall, thin and gray. Gray hair, gray eyebrows, gray eyes, gray mustache, silver-rimmed glasses, gray suit showing beneath white coat, even his skin looked gray . . .

"Feeling better?" asked Dr. Bascomb. At least his voice was definite. "You've had a scare, right? But the pain is gone, yes? The worst is over." He smiled down at Knute. Even his teeth looked gray. Involuntarily Knute groaned.

"Yes, yes, it is," Dr. Bascomb insisted. "What we'll do now is take some tests and provide you with help. Medication—maybe an anticoagulant drug that should reduce the risk of blood clots. Or a diuretic. No smoking. Do you smoke? No? Good. No salt. We'll look at your diet and exercise schedule and give you guidelines for those. And while you'll need to avoid sexual intercourse for four or five weeks, after that you can resume a full sex life if you wish." The gray smile came again. "That doesn't sound too bad, does it?"

The doctors all smiled and somebody laughed. I laughed, thought Knute. It's really funny. But now they're looking at me strangely so maybe I didn't laugh in the right place. Knute said, "No, it doesn't sound too bad. How long will I have to stay here?"

"That's always the next question," Dr. Bascomb chuckled. Yes, thought Knute, he really chuckled. Knute couldn't recall hearing anyone chuckling in front of him ever before. I am, he thought, thinking about things I never thought about. It's almost like a dream. Me—watching me.

"That depends on the tests," Dr. Guinness answered his question. "But if all goes well, I should think you could go home in a couple of days."

Now it was Dr. Bascomb's turn to listen through the stethoscope. He tapped Knute's chest. "This scar, caused by—ah—some sort of—accident some time ago?"

"You could say that. I was shot in the line of duty. Over twenty years ago."

"Hmmm. A great deal of stress in your line of work, I should think." He moved the stethoscope to another spot.

"Not so much here as in a high-crime area. Not enough to affect my heart. I wouldn't think my work would do that. Would it, Doc? I wouldn't want to quit working. I'm too young to quit working and law enforcement is all I know—"

"No, no, no. Don't even think about that. You're not going to be an invalid. There are too many things we can do these days, and too many ways you can help yourself, as well." Dr. Bascomb straightened and let the stethoscope dangle. The gray eyes looked kind. Maybe, Knute thought, he could believe this guy after all. God, how he hoped Bascomb was leveling with him. His son, his work, his life depended on this gray old man . . . "What do you say, Dr. Bell?" He'd known Bell a long time, surely he'd tell him the truth . . .

"Dr. Bascomb is aces, Knute." Doc Bell sounded a little awestruck. "You can go by whatever he says. All you've got to do is follow his lead."

"I'll do whatever you say, Doc." Suddenly he was tired, suddenly he wanted sleep, sleep where he didn't have to think about . . . Leif. "My boy, he's out in the hall."

"I'll have a little chat with him," said Dr. Bascomb. "Why don't you take a little rest?"

"Yes, yes. I'll do that. Yes."

And he did.

Dr. Bascomb thought Knute should stay home for a few days. "The rest of this week. Get things in order. You'd like that, wouldn't you? You impress me as a man who likes to organize things."

So Knute stayed home. Not in bed. Dr. Bascomb said he needn't stay in bed. "Just do what's comfortable. If you want to take a nap, take a nap. If you want to come downstairs, come downstairs. But don't run down! You know that. Common sense is prescribed in large amounts."

The first day wasn't so bad. He and Leif had a chance to talk, but not about Brenda. Nothing had been said about her or about that trashy magazine article. Maybe Leif hadn't even seen or heard about it. Knute's copy was at the police station and time had passed. It probably wasn't available at the supermarket anymore. There was a good chance Leif would never read it. That took a load off Knute's mind.

Leif told jokes to entertain him. Jokes he'd learned at camp. Like the one about the man and the lawn mower.

"There was this guy, Dad, who was a real nut when it came to having a perfect lawn. Every spare minute he had, he spent working on his lawn. He'd go out on his hands and knees and pull up every weed. He'd seed and fertilize and he'd water and he'd measure the length of a blade of grass to have it just so. He gave up his golf and his tennis and all his hobbies to concentrate on his lawn. He even neglected his wife and children.

"Now the neighbors noticed this and they began to make

jokes among themselves. 'Old Leon,' they'd say, 'he's a nut about that lawn. Crazy as a coot when it comes to grass. Just plain loony.'

"But they didn't really think he was crazy. Not until the day of the hurricane when they had to climb up on their roofs because of the storm. And down below they saw this straw hat moving back and forth in the water, back and forth, back and forth.

" 'Help, help!' they shouted. 'There's a man drowning down there.' But Mrs. Leon called from her upper window. 'That's nobody drowning,' she told them. 'That's Leon down there. He said he'd mow the lawn today come hell or high water.' "

Knute laughed dutifully.

"It was funnier when Arnie told it." Leif looked doubtful. "Maybe I left something out."

"It's all right," said Knute. "I thought it was pretty funny."

"Well, I've got another one that really is funny . . . There was this guy who . . ." He glanced away. "I think I forgot the punch line."

"Who told you all these jokes?" asked Knute. He guessed that last one hadn't been considered fit for fatherly consumption.

"The other counselors. Mostly Arnie Templar. He'd make a good stand-up comic, you know what I mean? Hey, there's the doorbell, I'll go see who it is."

He returned with Linda Maynard, who carried a pot of yellow chrysanthemums. "Hi, Knute. How are you?" She handed over the flowers. "I feel like we're going to a football game. Do you think the girls of today wear mums pinned to their jackets? I doubt it. You must be Leif. The last time I saw you, you were just a baby."

"The phone's ringing, Dad. I'll get it." Leif moved to the kitchen as if he was escaping.

Linda looked chagrined. "I was running off at the mouth, wasn't I? Sorry, Knute, I'm a little embarrassed. I thought maybe you'd be all alone and wanly reclining and I had an appointment with an avid house hunter in the neighborhood so I thought I'd stop in to give succor." She gestured toward the plant. "I picked that up at the supermarket. I just wanted to see how you are. Everybody's saying you nearly died."

"From what the doctors tell me—" He was interrupted by Leif telling him the phone was for him, should he tell her to call back?

"Her?"

"Officer Buono, she said."

"Oh. Maybe I'd better take it. Excuse me a minute, will you, Linda?"

"Oh, sure. I've got to go anyway. I've got a client waiting— You're going to be okay?"

"The doctors say so."

She smiled. "Wonderful. I'll keep in touch. Leif, don't bother to come to the door. 'Bye, boys." And she was gone.

Knute walked slowly into the kitchen. He'd discovered he was afraid to move, think or even talk fast. Damn, he felt like a weak, fragile old fool.

"Hello, Buono. What's up? Problems?"

"Hi, Chief. No problems, everything's fine. Lieutenant Beavers said to be sure and tell you there were no problems—that is, nothing we can't handle. I—I wonder if it would be all right if I came over to your house. There's something I want to talk about. If it's convenient. If it isn't, it can wait."

"Convenient? Sure, it's convenient. Listen, Buono, Alice, do me a favor. Bring all that stuff the people at Shangri-la wrote, will you? Mrs. dela Mare, Mrs. Meeny, Cullingham and Butler, all those papers. While I'm taking it easy here I'd like to go over them again. I don't think I ever got through all of them and I sure couldn't concentrate on them the way I wanted to. Will you do that? Please."

"Sure. I'll come along in a little while then. If you're sure it's okay."

"It's okay."

Leif, at the kitchen door, said, "You'll be talking police stuff, right? How about if I give the grass a good mow? Come hell or high water?" And he grinned.

Knute moved to put his arm around his son's shoulders. He suddenly realized how tall Leif had gotten. He was as tall as Knute himself. Sixteen years old and already as tall.

"Dad?"

"Uhmmm."

"I think I know how I blew it."

"Blew what?"

"The joke about the hat and the lawn mower. I didn't use an accent like Arnie. You see, it was a Polish joke."

Knute laughed.

When the doorbell rang Knute went to answer it himself. Instead of Alice Buono, Jenny Cobell stood on the porch, holding a large, cellophane-encased basket of fruit.

"Oh," said Knute.

"Oh," said Jenny, "I thought you'd be in bed."

Knute resisted a wild impulse to reply, "I could be if you'd like." It was just then that he realized he was getting better. "I've been told to move around," he said. "Won't you come in?" He gave a little wave to Leif, who stood watching by the idling lawn mower.

"We were terribly concerned when we heard of your illness." Jenny sat gracefully—long, slim legs crossed at the ankles in a perfect, ladylike pose.

"They say I can get back to work next week if I behave myself. In the meantime I'm doing some homework on the Shangri-la situation. Or I will be as soon as they bring over the papers. It's nice of you to drop by." It's also surprising, he thought; no, make that astonishing.

"I've a luncheon appointment today at the Inn so it was convenient. I'm pleased to hear your prognosis is so good. You can imagine our concern." She was wearing a suit of some crisp, lemon-colored material. Linen, he guessed. She had a very good figure and outstanding legs. He'd never really looked at her legs before, as she was always sitting behind that table at Town Hall.

"Can I get you some coffee?" He could manage that. There was instant coffee and powdered cream.

"No, thanks. As I said, I'm due at the Inn shortly." She indicated the fruit basket she'd set down on the marble-topped coffee table. "This is for you, of course. From the Board."

"Thanks."

She looked at him in that no-nonsense, let's-put-it-all-out-on-the-table way that she had. "Have you found out anything about that tabloid abomination?"

He shook his head. "I haven't had a chance to talk to anybody about it. This thing hit me like a ton of bricks, literally. I haven't heard either—are there repercussions? Lots of hollering?"

She shrugged. "About what we expected." The sun, streaming through the big window behind her, turned her fair hair into a halo. "What we're concerned about as much as anything is the implication that there's a lack of loyalty involved. To the town, as well as to you. I should think that would distress you the most."

"It does." But right now I don't want to talk about it or even think about it.

"Well"—she checked her watch and stood— "I've really got

to go. Keep in touch. Let us know how you are." She held out her hand. He shook it.

When they reached the door Alice Buono was standing on the other side of it, hand on the bell push. Knute introduced the two women and invited Alice in. Together they watched Jenny Cobell get into her white Mercedes and drive away. There was no sign of Leif out front but Knute could hear the sound of the lawn mower coming from the side yard. He needed to know where Leif was. It was a new feeling, this impression that everything and everybody was slightly out of orbit.

"I brought the Shangri-la papers." Officer Buono handed over a manila envelope. She didn't meet his eyes and he caught an odd expression on her face he'd never seen before. He thought fleetingly of distorted images on a scrambled TV channel.

"Chief," said Alice Buono, "there's something I have to tell you—"

The doorbell rang. Visitors' day at the Severson estate. "Excuse me," he said and went to see who it was. It was Dr. Guinness, picture-pretty in pale blue with a matching, broad-brimmed hat. "How are you feeling?" she asked. "Any problems?"

"I'm feeling all right." Knute pushed open the screen door. "Come in and join the party. Dr. Guinness, this is Officer Buono, she was just delivering some papers I wanted to look over. Papers concerning our friends at Shangri-la. I suppose it's okay to do a little headwork just to keep from going la-la."

Dr. Guinness looked amused. "I should think it was a good sign. I've come with news from Dr. Bascomb about your tests. So, if you can spare me a few minutes . . ."

"I'll go along now, Chief. Nice to have met you, Dr. Guinness." Alice backed her way out to the door.

"You wanted to discuss something," Knute reminded her.

"That's okay. I'll talk to you later."

"I hope I'm not interrupting anything." Dr. Guinness clearly doubted that anything could be more important than her information and no doubt she was right. Doctors, thought Knute, usually are. And usually think they are.

"Dr. Bascomb believes, and I concur, that you are out of risk for the time being." She smiled at him. "If you follow your new diet, exercise schedule and work schedule, things should go along very nicely. If there should be further trouble, he says we can consider angioplasty."

"And what is angioplasty?"

"It's an effective treatment for coronary artery disease when the coronary arteries are partially or totally closed. Yours are partially closed. That's what caused the attack, you see. Your heart wasn't getting its full quota of nutrients.

"Angioplasty is accomplished by inserting a narrow balloon through the circulatory system to the affected artery. This is done by attaching the balloon to a guiding catheter. When the balloon is placed at the narrowest part of the artery it's inflated at high pressure. This forces open the material that closed the artery, thus eliminating the need for bypass surgery. It can improve the quality of life with less time in the hospital and less cost. We're quite taken with it."

"What happens if it doesn't work?"

"Well, there's always bypass surgery. But let's not worry about any of that. We'll just keep tabs on you and you keep tabs on yourself and I feel certain—"

The phone rang. "Excuse me," he apologized, "this place has been like Route 9 at rush hour . . ." She nodded pleasantly and he went to the telephone.

"Knute, son, Lieutenant Beavers called us and don't you worry about a thing, we're planning on coming right away—"

"Hi, Dad. Hey, that's great but you don't really have to . . . I'm doing okay."

"Knute, I'm on the extension, what do you mean you're doing okay? Lieutenant Beavers said—"

"Hey, Mom. I'm really doing all right. One of my doctors is here now, I'll put her on the horn, she can tell you . . ."

And while Dr. Guinness was going through her heart's-full-quota-of-nutrients routine, Leif came in the kitchen escorting Ingrid and Inge, the In-House Cleaners. Knute had to grin at the expression on Leif's face when he was told that the gorgeous duo cleaned house for the Seversons. Not today, though. They were inquiring about Knute's health.

When everyone had finally gone, Leif asked the question, "Where did you find them, Dad? Where in the big wide world of pulchritudinous femalehood did you find them?"

Leif, Knute decided, was growing up.

Whereas he, Knute, was entering his second childhood.

Knute read:

Have you noticed how names have changed? Read the names on uniforms, on TV credit listings, or listen to the names of people you meet.

What happened to Jones and Smith? Where are the Joes, the Toms, the Susies and the Sallys?

Now we get Sean, spelled any of a hundred ways, and Kevin and Tyrone—has the whole world turned Irish? As for the girls, they tell me Jennifer and Ashley and Debbie and Kimberly have long replaced Mary and Betty and Catherine.

And the spellings. Consonants in juxtaposition with other consonants, vowels in odd places where vowels shouldn't be.

What's happened to names?

Don't give me that "a rose is a rose" stuff. I want a rose to be a rose. I want to know for certain what things are and who people are. I want words to mean what they meant. I want grammar used correctly. I want words spelled properly. I want words pronounced the way they should be. I want words, strong words.

Hero.

Lady.

Son.

Saint.

Killer.

He was walking away from me and I called his name. He

turned his head to face me; smiling, he turned his head. He kept walking while smiling at me.

He lost his head.

Hero. Lady. Son. Saint. Murderer. God.

Knute reread the final page of Ward Butler's ramblings before he placed it neatly in its pile. He still had to study the last of Cullingham's written recollections. All memories of his naval service that had been his life, it seemed. All but the first about his grandfather's death. Knute scanned the pages. Maybe Cullingham wasn't part of the pattern but there was something missing, something that should be there, Knute didn't know what exactly . . . He didn't recall reading this page.

As I said, the morning after word of the Jap surrender we left from Okinawa for Sasebo, Japan. We were the first American ship in Sasebo since the late thirties. About a week later we were sent to Nagasaki. We had been told that we had dropped a big bomb there a couple of weeks before. The city had disappeared, was just leveled. A few walls and partial structures were all that was visible.

The USS *Wichita* was there. We were to maintain a twenty-four-hour watch with an LCVP to keep Japanese boats from getting too close. We didn't know what they would do. I drew the midnight-to-four watch with a gunner's mate who carried a carbine. We ventured up the river, which was off limits, to get a closer look at the city. It was barely daylight and we could see very little in the heavy morning mist. I managed to get the boat hung up on something and couldn't get it free in spite of working it back and forth. I think it was something like a steel beam sticking up from the bottom. Anyway, we sweated it and finally I managed to get us free and out of the river before we were

spotted by the flagship *Wichita* because, as I said, this river was
OFF LIMITS. Later I found out it wasn't a river but a narrow,
deep-cut bay at the meeting point of the Nomo and Nishi-
Sonogi peninsulas.

And just as we were triumphantly sailing out of this no-
man's-land the sun came up in earnest and I saw a reddish haze
over what was once the Mitsubishi miniature-submarine boat-
yard. I saw black, upright skeletons of girders and beyond that,
rubble in the red haze, the rust-colored mist, but no people.
What happened to the people?

I wanted to talk it over with Wally but I couldn't. I'd last seen
him nearly a month ago. We were anchored in the Whangpoo,
Wally's ship and my ship, a surprise, a really big surprise, and I
used the LCVP to pick him up and take us ashore. We tied her
up at the dock and made our way over a little footbridge that
spanned a canal. Shanghai. We'd never been in Shanghai before.
Guys on the ship said there was this little bar over the bridge
and around the corner. They spoke English there, they said. I
said, "Shanghai is an English port, isn't it? Shouldn't everybody
speak English?" Phipps, who was giving me the word, said he
didn't know. China was China but at this place he could guarantee they spoke English. With a Chinese accent.

It didn't look like much from the outside, but if Phipps and
the guys said it was okay we figured it must be all right, so we
went in. There were some Limey sailors and some of our guys
from other ships so we figured it was the right place. There
were some girls, too, Chinese and Caucasian even. There was a
jukebox playing songs like Vera Lynn's "We'll Meet Again." The
record was kind of scratchy.

We had some beers. We struck up conversations with some of
the other ratings. We had some more beers. Next thing I knew,

two of the Caucasian girls were in a booth with us. White Russians, they said they were.

Wally had had more to drink than I had and all of a sudden I started to get nervous. My girl, or at least the girl sitting on my side of the booth, said something insulting about the U.S.A. I asked her to repeat that and she did. I was holding her hand at the time and I began to squeeze her hand hard, so hard I could feel the bones move. I think I might have broken it. She grabbed a heavy glass ashtray and hit me with it. She caught me over the eyebrow, just missing the eye itself. All hell was breaking loose. People were yelling and hitting each other and hitting me and I was hitting back.

I heard the Shore Patrol's whistle. I guess the owner of the bar must have called them. I said, "Wally, let's get out of here," but he didn't answer. I looked down at him. He was lying on the floor inside the booth we'd been sitting in. "Wally," I said again and touched him.

He didn't move.

He was dead.

Somebody had stuck a knife into him.

I'll never forget that night or that place.

In Shanghai.

Knute sighed. Yes, Cullingham was part of the pattern. Whatever the pattern was. He had to talk to him. He had to talk to Mrs. Butler. Then, maybe, it would make more sense.

Roseanna dela Mare.

Evangeline Meeny.

Ward Butler.

Bill Cullingham. But Bill Cullingham was alive and kicking so maybe he'd better get out to Shangri-la right away. Surely it wouldn't hurt him to sit and listen to somebody. But perhaps he shouldn't drive. He'd get someone to drive him.

Alice Buono. She'd been in on it since the beginning so she'd be more help than anyone else.

Besides—what was it she wanted to talk to him about? God, he hoped the girl hadn't gone and gotten herself pregnant. She wouldn't be that stupid, would she? Surely not.

Sitting beside her in the black Chrysler he asked, "What was it you were going to tell me? You've got my full attention now so let's hear it."

She looked at him out of the corners of her blue eyes. "I found that—that copy of a magazine on your desk . . ."

Oh, so that was it, thought Knute. "Did you read the garbage about Wellesley?"

"I— Yes, I did."

"Yeah? Well, I guess you know a lot of it's lies . . . What did you do with it? Filed it in the wastebasket, I hope."

"Oh, I didn't touch it. I just left it there. I wouldn't disturb anything on your desk."

"You can't let something like that story shake you up." What had she thought of the innuendo about Brenda? Jesus, if he could just get his hands on the perpetrator of that piece of trash.

"It was horrible. Simply horrible." She was facing the road, watching where she drove, but he thought he saw a teardrop at the edge of her eye. She really was distressed. He felt a new surge of anger.

"Damn," he said, "when I get my hands on the guy who set that thing up, he'll be out on his—ear. I'd give my eyeteeth to be wrong on that score but that's what it looks like. They were tales right from the police blotter—but never mind. It'll all blow

over. The only people who'll remember are me and the blabber-
mouth, whoever he may be."

"I'd call the informant something worse. An idiot, a gross
fool." She braked to turn into the Shangri-la roadway. "A sorry
piece of shit."

That jolted him. It's my age, he thought. I'm just not used to
nice girls using bad language. He had no reply other than agree-
ment. If she'd been a young male cop he could have chimed in.

"Take a right here, will you? We'll stop off at the Butler place
first. Then Cullingham's. And finally, the Ventress woman.
While chasing wild geese, might as well go for the whole flock."

"You've got some kind of theory?"

"An idea. That's all. A fuzzy idea. Take notes for me, please.
About all I'm good for is talking."

"Wait," she said when she'd stopped in front of the Butler
cottage.

He paused in unbuckling his seat belt. "Yes?"

"Here's your papers." She thrust the manila envelope at him.
"What's wrong, Buono? Something else bothering you?"

She sighed and pushed open her door. "Everything's bothering me. It's that time of the month."

Speechless, he followed her up the walk.

Amanda Butler wore mourning of sorts—black cotton pants and a black T-shirt with white polar bears printed on it. She looked surprised and said, "Oh, I thought you were Bill. Bill Cullingham. There's a meeting of the residents at the Center. He's going to take me." She glanced at her wristwatch. "He should have been here by now. The meeting's at ten."

"Come on." Knute grabbed Alice by the hand and hurried her off the stoop, down the walk to the car. "We've got to get to Alpha square right away."

"Slow down," she protested, "slow down."

He hardly heard her.

No one answered Cullingham's bell. Knute thought he should break a window to get in and was ready to do that when Alice said she heard sounds from behind the cottage. There they found the man watering his rosebushes. Knute sat down on a wrought-iron bench, listening to his heartbeat.

"Mrs. Butler is worried about you," Alice explained. "She's expecting you to take her to a meeting."

Cullingham grimaced. "To tell you the truth, I just don't want to go. Amanda kind of roped me into taking her so I guess I'll have to pick her up. They'll just say all the usual crap, you know, like we need more police protection and who's responsible for these awful deaths. I can ask myself those questions right here at home. When I moved here I thought I was buying security. You okay, Chief Severson? You look kind of pale."

"He's been in the hospital," Alice told him, then stopped in mid-sentence when Knute made a gesture. "For a checkup."

"Come in where it's cool," Cullingham offered. "You wanted to see me about something? I can call Amanda and tell her I'm tied up. Then I won't have to go to that darn coffee klatch."

Knute said he did want to talk to him and asked if he would please tell Mrs. Butler to stay put because they'd be back in a little while. Inside it was cool. He commented on it when Cullingham got off the phone. Not many houses in New England went in for air-conditioning; there was no need for it most of the time. Cullingham agreed. "But they fixed these places up with all the creature comforts and to tell you the truth, I don't mind. I can take a little coddling in my old age. But you folks didn't come here to talk about air-conditioning, and this pretty little lady hasn't taken a notebook out to write about that. You came to talk about Ward Butler, I'd guess. Do I think he committed suicide? Maybe. Or maybe it was an accident. We were friends, yes, but not buddy-buddy. We didn't have that much in common. Ward went to Harvard and I only had a high school diploma. Course that don't matter so much when you get to be our age but it kind of sets the tone of a relationship, if you know what I mean. Like when we'd read the newspaper, I'd read the front page and the sports, the comics and maybe the editorial page. Ward would read the theatre reviews, stories on the ballet and the art world, and then he'd go on to the rest of it."

Knute opened his manila envelope. "I've been reading your autobiography."

"Oh? Delilah gave you that, did she?" Cullingham looked down at the floor. "I'm not much of a writer." He looked up. "Why would you be interested in that?"

"I read Mrs. dela Mare's, too. And Mrs. Meeny's. Also Mr.

Butler's. Trying to get an idea as to why these three died so suddenly—and so close together in time."

"No telling what gets into a person's head, is there? But you should know that things like that happen in threes. Every time some big shot dies, usually two more kick off right about the same time. I guess nature or God or whatever you call it likes to have things done in threes." He grinned mirthlessly. "Like the leaves on poison ivy."

"You think it was just a coincidence then? Your close friend Roseanna? Your acquaintance Mrs. Meeny? Your not-so-close friend Ward Butler?"

He shrugged. "You got a better idea?"

"I'm working on one. Like you said, there's no telling what gets into a person's mind. Tell me about this fella Wally. The one who was killed in Shanghai."

Cullingham looked him in the eye. "What about him? He was just a shipmate. A million years ago."

"He's just about the main character in your memoirs."

"We were just kids, went to sea together. You're all alone out there. It's a big ocean, so you get close to somebody when you can." He frowned. "What happened then's got nothing to do with now."

Maybe not. Knute's idea was so tenuous he had nothing to aim at, no target. "You said it—it kind of sets the tone. What about your late wife? You don't mention her at all."

"I never got to that part. Margaret was a wonderful woman. She died of the big C. It was bad, that's all there is to it. Listen, if you've got some kind of crazy bee in your bonnet that I had anything to do with them dying, all I can tell you is I didn't. I had nothing to do with their deaths." He voice was under control but his face had reddened.

Knute shook his head. "I just want to make sure you don't

join the party." Alice glanced up from her notebook, startled. But then she hadn't read all the stories he had.

"Me?" Cullingham stood up, hands on hips. "What makes you think anything will happen to me?"

Knute gave him a long look. "You'll be careful, won't you? These next few days. Don't let anybody talk you into anything."

Cullingham stared back at him, then laughed.

"Nothing's going to happen to me," he said.

"You're sure?"

"I'm sure. Nothing's going to happen to me."

"Mrs. Butler, your husband wrote some pages for Miss Ventress' writing class. Did he show them to you?"

Amanda Butler shook her neat gray head. "He wouldn't. Ward was a very private person. I was surprised when he joined the writing class. But I suppose he was bored and looking for a challenge. It was hard for Ward to do nothing, you know. He'd always been such an active person, both physically and intellectually."

"Much of what he writes is subjective. He talks about beauty. And pain. And death. The death of a cat named Charlie."

"Charlie. Yes." She smiled wistfully. "Such a dear animal. We never had another after Charlie. We both took his death rather hard, and decided we didn't need that kind of thing again."

Knute referred to the Butler papers. "There's one paragraph —he wrote: 'He was walking away from me and I called his name. He turned his head to face me; smiling, he turned his head. He kept walking while smiling at me. He lost his head.' Can you tell me who he was writing about, or what that means?"

Mrs. Butler lost her gentle smile. "That would be—I think it must have been—that was Phillip. Our son, Phillip." Her voice roughened. "He died in an accident. A long time ago. Thirty-four years ago."

"I don't like to bring back unhappy memories, but what—"

"You aren't bringing back memories, Chief Severson, they're always there. It's just that I was able to take it much better than Ward because I wasn't there to see it happen, and he was." She folded her hands in her lap and looked up at him. "Phillip was taking flying lessons, you see. We weren't too happy about it. He was young, but he was keen on becoming a pilot. Ward had driven him to the little airport where they gave lessons. Phillip had checked the plane out with his instructor, who then started the engine, and Phillip was about to get into the plane when Ward called out to him, 'Good luck, son.' Phillip turned to answer him and walked into the propeller. Ward was never able to forget that. You can understand why."

Knute nodded. He waited until he was sure she had her emotions under control. "Do you think your husband might have taken his own life, Mrs. Butler?"

She sighed. "I can't be sure. I hope not, but I can't be sure. In recent years Ward grew less and less communicative. We just didn't talk much to each other about our feelings. To tell you the truth, I didn't mind so very much. After a number of years you tend to tire of reassuring someone . . . perhaps the loss of communication was my fault but whoever was to blame didn't matter, it was a fait accompli. So I'm afraid I can't tell you what my husband was thinking that morning with the gun. Accident or suicide, I just don't know."

"And there was no one else around? You're certain of that?"

Her eyes widened, narrowed. "I was here, Chief Severson. But no one else."

It was his turn to sigh.

"If you want to find out what was on Ward's mind," Mrs. Butler went on, "I suggest you talk to Delilah Ventress. He spent a lot of time over there and they must have talked about something."

Delilah Ventress wasn't home. They could hear the poodle barking from behind the locked front door but nobody answered Knute's rapping. "She must be at that meeting," he decided. "We can wait for her in the car."

"It's kind of hot in the car." Alice picked at a button on her uniform jacket.

"It's about time we got cooler weather. There's an umbrella table and some chairs on her patio. How about there?" Buono was being testy. That wasn't like her.

"I hope she won't mind."

He was about to snap "Why should she mind?" but Buono was heading for the umbrella so he shut up and followed her.

They sat in silence. Knute studied the flower beds. Zinnias he recognized; a bee buzzed a taller bloom—snapdragon? Birds sang and the breeze rustled the leaves on the trees. There was no noise from traffic. It was all rather restful until Buono said, "Chief?"

"Hmmm?" He had let his eyelids droop.

"I was the one who told Brad Preston all those stories." She waited for his response and when none came she went on. "In the *International Interviewer*. I don't know why I rattled on so— yes, I do. I wanted to impress him, to interest him, to prove that my job was important, that *I* was important."

Slowly he stood, his back turned to her.

She cleared her throat. "You see, he was so sharp, so— He was like a guy in the movies with his Jaguar and his clothes and the way he looked and talked . . . he was so slick, he'd been everywhere and I couldn't figure out why he was so interested in me." Her tone hardened. "I know now, of course, but I didn't think for a minute that he would print the things I told him . . . I exaggerated a little, too, you know, the way you do just to make a story better . . ." Her voice trailed off.

He turned to face her. She looked like a child waiting to be spanked. Trust, he thought. When you've been a cop for such a long time, it's hard to trust. You're always just a little suspicious, always wondering what's really underneath the words, the gestures. Not just with those you should be wary of but with everybody. Maybe Brenda sensed that. Maybe that was why . . . Little threads of trust, so thin, so fragile, had been spun around Alice Buono. An embryo spiderweb of trust, now brushed away. "Take the car," he said, "and go back to the station. Send someone to get me. Whoever's handy, I don't care."

She blinked uncertainly. "But, what—"

"Go back to the station and wait."

She picked up her shoulder bag and notebook and got to her feet. He watched her walk slowly to the car. He thought she was crying. He didn't give a damn.

Delilah Ventress rode up on a three-wheeled bicycle that looked like an adult tricycle. "Well," she said when she saw him, "I've been wondering when you'd come around. But didn't I hear you were ill?"

"A temporary upset," he told her. "You were expecting me?"

"Of course. Sooner or later." She parked the bicycle by her garage door. "My TV show is on for the next thirty minutes. We'll watch that and then talk. Come on in, it's hot out here."

The poodle greeted her ecstatically. Fifi was the poodle's name, if he remembered correctly. Fifi had a yellow bow in her fur to match her mistress' outfit. Delilah cooed at the dog to settle it down and then turned on the television. Vanna White grinned out at him as the screen lit up with "Wheel of Fortune." Knute felt like commanding, "Turn that thing off, this is serious, this is a murder investigation" . . . but he wasn't at all certain it was a murder investigation and besides he'd lost his confidence in recent days—he'd lost his authority . . .

He watched the three contestants trying to guess words. Knute knew the answers before they did. Yeah, sure, he thought, I know all the answers.

When Pat Sajak told the winner to wave to America out of the window of her new car, Delilah turned the set off. "I hope you didn't mind, but that's my favorite show. I just love Pat Sajak. Now, how about some iced tea? I keep a container full in the refrigerator. Sun tea. I make it by setting it out in the sun. It won't take but a minute."

Laid back, that's what he'd be; the thing to do was to be laid back, so he'd swill iced tea for a while with a little yellow gnome of a woman wearing a light brown wig. While she was gone, the poodle following at her heels, he separated his papers into little piles.

"Sugar, lemon?" asked Delilah, returning with a tray.

He shook his head. "Plain. What did you mean, I'd come calling sooner or later?"

She smiled and patted her neat curls. "If you wanted answers, you'd come. Of course, if you were lazy or stupid you wouldn't, but I didn't think you were lazy or stupid. A little slow, perhaps, but thorough. That's the way I figured you."

He stared at her. She looked like such a silly little old lady. "It took me a while to see the connection. The deaths. They all had someone die on them. In different times, in different places, from different causes. For different reasons. That's the connection, isn't it? It has to be."

She pursed her mouth. Her upper lip was scored by tiny vertical wrinkles. Old-age cracks. What caused that? he wondered. The juice has gone—that must be it—and she is becoming, slowly, a mummy. "Do you know about guilt?" she asked. The dog jumped into her lap and arranged itself.

"Yes." Oh, yes.

She studied him. "You probably know something of guilt personally, I can see that in you, but you're not old enough to know what happens to guilt over the years. It is born, of course, when you think you've done something wrong, something 'bad' as we used to say when we were kids. 'I've been bad,' we think, but we love ourselves so we can't accept the bad deed. We blame someone else and push the guilt into a mental closet, shove it in there, stuff it in there and slam the door!"

The dog looked up at Delilah, then watched Knute with beady eyes. Delilah took a swallow of tea.

"This works pretty well for a long time. Oh, once in a while we open the door just a little crack to see if the guilt's still there —if it's hale and hearty, or fading away; but if it was a good strong guilt it's still breathing hard, so we slam the door once more and get on with life.

"But—comes a day when there isn't so much life to get on with and then we begin to dwell on yesterday rather than tomorrow. We begin remembering. At least we *think* we're remembering but what we recall isn't always fact. Still, that doesn't matter so much. We remember wonderful times, times when we were all that we ever hoped we could be. We remember old friends and, if we can, go to visit them, for they are the only ones who know who we are. Not that fat old woman with the cane but that young, sprightly girl with the sunny smile. We don't have to tell them that we didn't always look and act like this—they know it and so it's nice to be with old friends. But you kind of forget exactly why you became friends in the first place so you look back and wonder why you needed them then. Because that's what friendship is, you know, supplying a need."

He wanted to hurry her up, to tell her to get to the point, but again he was powerless. He'd just have to sit there and let her ramble on. That's what old people do, he thought, they get started on one subject and they wander off on another and they just go on and on . . . until they say something.

She shifted her weight, gave the poodle a pat, took another sip of tea. Her hands and face were spotted with brown flecks. Years in the sun had done that . . . "Supplying a need," she repeated. "God, we are so selfish, aren't we? No matter. Continue, Delilah. You're boring the young man. It's about this time that life itself gets boring and, having little else to do, we take a little peek behind that closet door. Guilt is just as strong as ever but we're not, so we don't get the door shut quite as tightly and guilt begins to ooze out around the cracks and through the keyhole. The next thing we know is, voilà! Guilt is with us, sitting beside us on the sofa watching television." She raised her arms and made fists of her spotted little hands.

"You're telling me that guilt was the motive for these deaths?"

She nodded her curly head and brought her arms down to caress Fifi. "But of course. That's the connection you found. Guilt. Roseanna, Evangeline, Ward, they killed themselves because of guilt. Guilt they'd shut away and never dealt with. I thought you knew. I thought it was obvious."

"Guilty of what? Did Mrs. dela Mare kill her husband . . ."

Delilah ran her finger around Fifi's collar and the dog tags jingled. "Roseanna had more guilt than anyone. She was a collector of guilts, that lady. First there was her family guilt and then there was her husband guilt and then her son guilt. She was a very strong woman, Roseanna, it was all her idea in the first place. The others just listened and nodded."

"So she did kill herself?"

"Oh, yes."

"But the light bulb outside the door? The blood on her hands? Signs that she tried to escape?"

"She fixed the light bulb so that no one would come to her rescue. And of course she tried to get out. Survival is stronger than guilt in the long run. She knew that, so she loosened the bulb. She chose the long way to die, then she ensured her passing. As I said, a very strong woman."

"So she did kill her husband?"

"No, no. She just made him miserable. Miserable enough to— Well, she told me that the boat accident occurred when he was loaded with sleeping pills. They hushed that up, of course. She said she could never be certain whether he died from an accident or by his own hand. She didn't much care but she didn't want suicide talked about. Not even in the case of her own death. Scandal, you know. We old folks don't like scandal."

"Didn't she love her husband?"

"I don't think Roseanna was capable of loving anyone, not since her mother died. I think she just put a great big sealing patch over the love part and let it die from lack of oxygen. That's what's wrong with Gordon, the son. He can't be a husband and father because his mother didn't teach him to love. It's because he *can't* be a husband and father that his wife can't be a sober mother and so the little girl will . . . You see how it goes on and on?"

"She told you all these things?" He was incredulous.

"Oh, yes. That's part of the guilt. One must confess to somebody. She saved the worst part till last."

"The worst?"

"The mass murder of her family. She did it, you know. She took the silver nitrate from her stepfather's darkroom and laced the lemonade for the picnic. She swore to me that she believed he alone would drink the lemonade. The others preferred tea, she claimed, but I don't quite believe that. Still, she was young and she thought like a child . . . I said she never loved after her mother died. I take that back. I think it happened when her mother remarried. I think she began to hate then, first the step-father, then the mother—or would it be the other way around? —and finally the entire family because they accepted him."

He flipped through the memoir pages. "But she wasn't there when they died. She was off on her honeymoon."

"She didn't have to be there. She left very early that morning but she knew the picnic equipment. She knew they transported the lemonade in a fancy thermos bottle. They had two of them: brown for tea, blue for lemonade. She put the poison in the empty blue thermos. Then when the beverage was poured in—" She made a gesture and the dog, startled from its nap, jumped up and barked.

"She told you all this? Of her own free will?"

"Oh, yes. I repeat: sooner or later, guilt must have its say."

She looked so—grandmotherly sitting there with her big, clear eyes and her plump, soft face and her curly wig the color of peanut butter. How many dreadful secrets did that wig cover? Mentally he shook himself. He was getting mesmerized.

"Mrs. Meeny—guilt there, too? The husband and the carbon monoxide? Don't tell me she booby-trapped the car."

The doorbell rang, breaking the spell. "Who can that be?" wondered Miss Ventress. The poodle jumped from her lap and ran to the door yapping.

"Someone for me, I think. I'll answer it." He had to hold the

dog back by its collar. Officer Hersholt stood on the little porch.
"Buono said I should come pick you up."

"When I'm ready," said Knute. "Just wait until I'm ready."
Back in his chair, when the dog had stopped barking, he pushed
her to continue talking. "Mrs. Meeny?"

"Evangeline Meeny wouldn't have the least idea how to dis-
connect an air hose on a car any more than I would. She
wouldn't have had to stoop to such manipulations had she
wanted her husband dead, which she didn't. She could drive a
man to suicide simply by being Evangeline. Which is what she
did, of course. She never did come out and admit that, but
surely you can read between the lines of what she wrote. She
was a pathological liar, you know. Wouldn't recognize the truth
if it jumped up and bit her."

"Then why would she kill herself? That is, if she believed
what she wrote, that his death was an accident?"

Delilah nodded her wig wisely. "That's what guilt does. It
cuts through the camouflage. It says, 'Hey! You did this, don't
kid yourself. You're responsible.' All these years, deep down she
knew. She knew just how she drove him to it. Until finally, the
guilt became bigger than she was and bingo!"

"So she told you she was going to drown herself?" He knew
he sounded skeptical. How had she come up with all this information? Some kind of moral blackmail?

"Oh, yes. She said it would be the easiest way. I said it might
not work. The human body has a tendency to float to the surface. I told her if she were a swimmer she would know you have
to work at staying under. She said she'd take care of that. She'd
fasten her seat belt and the wheelchair would hold her down."

He frowned. "She impressed me as the kind of old lady who'd
never give up."

Delilah looked thoughtful. "I felt that way, too. Possibly she was goaded into it by the fact that her son was having difficulty in keeping her here. He isn't wealthy, you know."

He had to believe it—in a distorted way it made sense. "But if they told you what they planned to do, why didn't you try to stop them? Notify Bancroft? The families? Somebody?"

She shrugged. "I don't play God. When you get to be my age you realize you can't change people. Besides, Evangeline was a liar. I didn't believe her. At the time."

Just a cuddly little old lady with cutesy curls, a beribboned poodle and a sympathetic ear. She made his flesh crawl. "And I suppose Ward Butler laid out his plans for your approval, too."

"Not really. Ward was a secretive man by nature. A very private person. A very troubled man, as well. I'm sure you could see that from his writings. I knew he would take his life—I just didn't know how or when. He didn't seek my advice."

"His guilt was the accidental death of his son. He didn't cause the death, it was an out-and-out accident—"

"They'd had a quarrel, I know that much. Ward was a prime example of the old school and his son was a product of a more permissive time so strife was inevitable."

"You sound like a book." Knute scowled at her.

She smiled her grandmotherly smile. "I do, don't I? Sorry, it's an occupational disease. At any rate they had this argument. Ward shouted the boy's name, forbade him to go up in the plane, ordered him home immediately, that sort of thing, and the boy only smiled and walked into the propeller. One can imagine the shock."

Yes, one could. "What about Bill Cullingham? Is he a candidate? Was his guilt caused by the death of his friend? Or his wife? In either case, why?"

"Both, I think. Bill was the one who took his friend to that bar in Shanghai and then, later, his wife died from cancer of the uterus. Both victims, as he sees it, of his sexual appetites."

"Sexual appetites?"

She nodded. "He felt a homosexual attraction to his friend Wally. When he conquered that and went 'straight' his wife's cancer occurred in that part of the body associated with sex. He felt he caused it, a retribution for his sins, something along those lines."

"He needs to see a psychiatrist. Somebody who can help. All of these people, they needed help. You knew that. Why didn't you do something? How's your conscience on aiding and abetting? How's *your* guilt?"

"Oh, but I did do something. I listened and I commiserated. That's all anyone can do, you know. I think Bill is coping with his guilt these days. He seems better to me at least. I like to think I'm responsible for that. I do believe I'll have another glass of tea. Will you join me?"

There must be something he could charge her with. Aiding and abetting suicide—what was the law on that? Could he prove it? "I can charge you with collusion." He wasn't sure he could; he wasn't sure of anything.

She stood and drew herself up to her full five feet. The poodle pranced around her. "I merely acted as a friend. I never committed a crime in my life."

"Three people are dead, yet you don't feel any guilt?"

"Certainly not."

"How many other potential suicides among your 'writing students' are there?" He could at least warn Bancroft and force him to cancel all her writing classes. That would take care of the sanctioned get-togethers but what about the private ones? What could he do to keep people from killing themselves? Stop! Stop in the name of the law! Stop or I'll arrest you? And no matter what she said, could he believe her? After all, wasn't her whole life a matter of fiction? He heard her say something about how the others had lives as dull as dishwater. He got to his feet. He felt tired. Maybe he was doing too much. He'd go home and take it easy for the rest of the day . . .

"Don't go away mad," said Miss Ventress coyly. "Stay and have some more tea. Maybe you'd like to talk about *your* guilt?"

"Guilt? I'm like you. I don't have any guilt." And he left without so much as a good-bye.

School started and nothing new happened at Shangri-la and Knute began to feel better. He had a long talk with Alice Buono.

Dr. Bascomb said he was doing well and if he kept it up there'd be no need for surgery of any kind. Inge and Ingrid began cooking casseroles on the days they came to clean. They were pretty good cooks. Leif announced he'd like to learn to be a chef.

Jenny Cobell invited Knute to speak at a meeting of the Wellesley Club. He was flabbergasted and nervous as hell but they laughed at his humor, applauded his speech and generally made him feel like one of the gang. Since the gang at the Wellesley Club included the movers and shakers of Wellesley, being one of the gang wasn't bad. Nobody said anything about *International Interviewer,* not a word.

He got up the nerve to ask Jenny Cobell to dinner. She said she couldn't on the night he named but could she take a rain check? He said sure and maybe one day he'd dare to ask her again.

Christmas would have been a real drag but he and Leif flew down to Florida and ate his mother's turkey and went to Walt Disney World along with a million other people.

Alice Buono started dating Harry Hersholt and that caused a lot of heavy humor at the station. "We're just good friends," Alice told Knute in seeming sincerity. "I like him better than Ricky Cappabianco." That mystified Knute but he took it in stride. He was taking a lot of things in stride these days; he'd decided to let nothing ripple his smooth surface.

Miss Fancy Evans and Mr. Robert Bancroft announced their engagement in the Wellesley *Townsman*. The wedding was scheduled for June.

Linda Maynard had a canoe. She invited Knute to join her on a canoe ride on the Charles come spring. "I haven't been in a canoe for a hundred years," he told her, bemused.

"Canoe canoe?" asked Linda, making a silly face.

"Sure. I'm a pretty good paddler. Or used to be. Can I bring lunch?"

"It will be easier for me to do that. You can bring a bottle of wine. We'll get tipsy and sing sea chanteys."

Leif made the baseball team at the high school. That was a surprise because he was only a sophomore.

The Red Sox won their opening-day game. Then they lost the next three.

A Japanese runner won the Boston Marathon.

Knute looked around and it was May and he realized he'd been going through a period of healing. Leif needed new clothes for camp; he'd be going back as a senior counselor and he'd grown two inches taller and had gained twenty pounds.

They went to Jordan Marsh to buy the clothes. Passing through the book department, Knute noticed that Delilah Ventress had a new book out. It was on a table titled "Recent Bestsellers." He picked one up and glanced inside.

The book began: "I was born in a root cellar in the midst of a cyclone. I'm told the cyclone was ferocious and the root cellar crowded. My mother was there, of course, and her mother and her mother's mother and my mother's sisters, Lucy and Loretta. You will immediately observe that there were no men present. There were various reasons for this but the main one was that the women in our family always outlived the men . . ."

He looked at the cover of the book. *Guilty as Sin* by Delilah Ventress. He looked at the back of the book. There was her picture.

"Hey, Dad, over this way," Leif was calling him.

He knew now what Delilah Ventress reminded him of—a toad wearing a wig. A venomous toad wearing a wig. Maybe he could talk Gordon dela Mare into charging her with plagiarism. "Miss," he said to the salesperson, "how much is this book?"

Disgruntled, he paid $18.95 for a piece of evidence. The prices they charged—but never mind. "Gosh, Dad," said Leif, "what did you buy that for?"

Why did he buy it? Something solid? Something he could hold up as proof of wrongdoing? "I'm going to give it to someone if I can," he answered. "I'm really going to give it to her."

If I can.

ABOUT THE AUTHOR

TOBIAS WELLS is a pseudonym of a prolific writer of mystery novels who also writes for the Crime Club under the name Stanton Forbes. She currently resides in Sanford, Florida.